THE SECRET SU

and other stories

By Duncan Harley

Supported by The Doric Board

By the same author:

The A-Z of Curious Aberdeenshire
The Little History of Aberdeenshire
Long Shadows – Tales of Scotland's North East
The Poetry Mannie – The Doric Poetry of Bob Smith

"I don't like the looks of it," said the King "however, it may kiss my hand, if it likes."
"I'd rather not," the Cat remarked.

Dod King, collector of tales and one-time librarian at the Invermorrisay Public Lending Library.

CONTENTS

SPRING - CAAL AN WAIRMER WEET WIKS

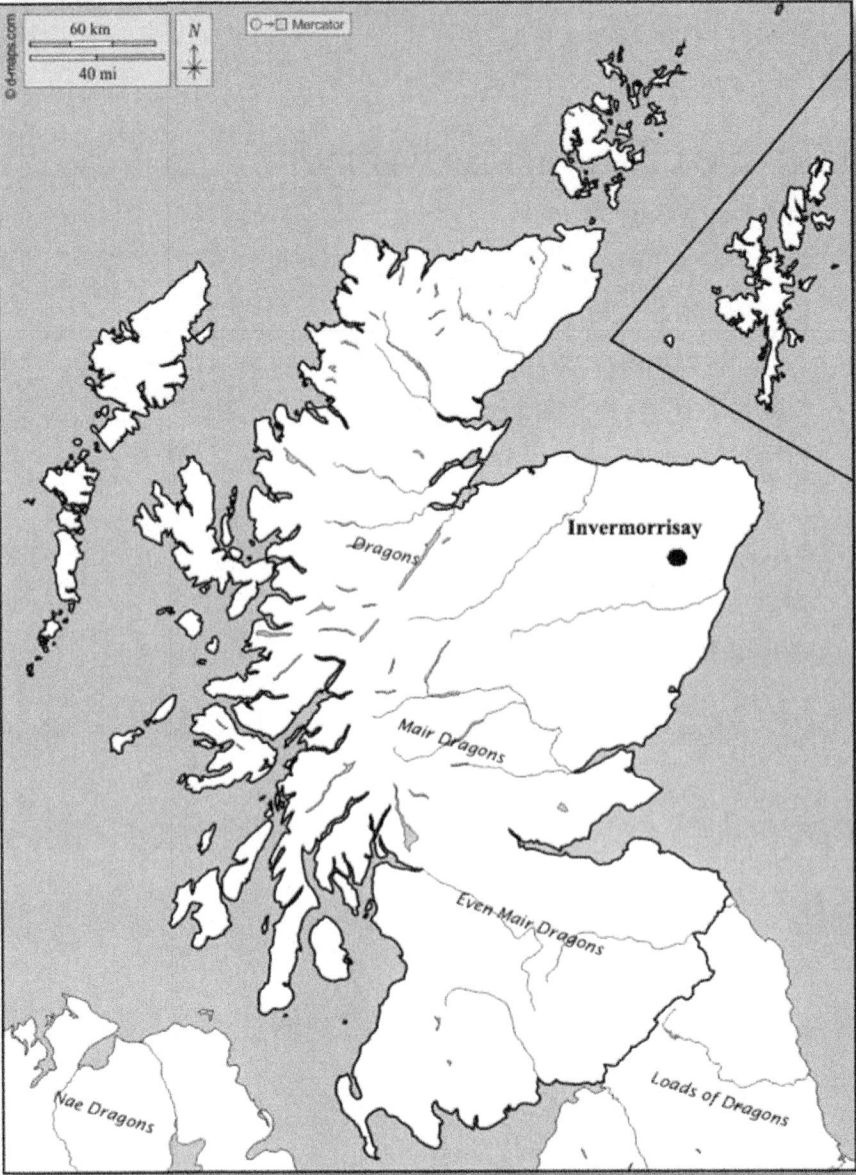

INTRODUCTION

I first stumbled across Dod and his bunch of cronies as a newcomer to Aberdeenshire in the middle of the 1980s. It was a good time for incomers to the oil rich North East and a trip to the local lending library where Dod King was employed was never a chore. Often as not the man would stop what he was supposed to be doing and regale you with tales of who was doing what with who and where they were doing it. About who was on the take and about whatever local scandal was on the whispering circuit. If you were unlucky, he would spin you a libelous joke about some local worthy or other in full earshot of the entire library. If you were lucky, he would whisper it in a conspiratorial manner which would at least allow you to snigger unnoticed. Of course, he never let on that he was writing it all down. That would only be revealed long after his death.

In those far-off days, the extraction of the black black oil was in full swing and the North East of Scotland was a land of golden opportunity. Jobs were plentiful and house prices seemed affordable. The roads across Aberdeenshire and Moray and the Mearns were chock full of shiny new cars and there were few if any potholes along the main roads for folk to gripe on about. The sun always shone, it never rained and tummle-doon farm cottages ripe for renovation were at chape-john prices and you could rent a damp cottar hoose for jellybeans. It was all about to change. But neither the tenants nor the landlords, mainly ordinary hard-working farmers, had any real inkling about the ups and downs of the offshore energy industry or the ebb and flow of a barrel of oil. These heady days are lang awa but Dod King's wee scribblins provide a gateway to that past.

For the sake of some measure of clarity, I have ordered Dod's tales into seasonal headings - Summer, Autumn, Winter and Spring - and included his original dates amongst the individual chapter headings. Presumably these relate to when he penned the stories and, in the fullness of time, maybe another dusty suitcase full of his wirds will turn up to help resolve the puzzle of the dates.

Many of the tales are set in the fictional Garioch toon of Invermorrisay. Some are set further afield. One or two emanate from the slopes of Ben

Aucherie, a fictional hill range held dear by the folk of Aberdeenshire.

There is no evidence that very many of Dod's tales were widely published, although at this distance in time you just never can tell. One or two did end up in the local newspapers as All Fools Day spoof articles and they are repeated here in the tale titled *The Library Service All Fools Day Story Competition*. Maybe further examples of Dod's published stories will come to light one of these days.

A good few of the characters in this collection appear in several of the tales. Others just the once. Some stories, such as *Musical Box* and *Practical Airship Handling*, relate directly to the workplace. Whereas others, such as *The One-Armed Bandit, Cody's Gran, Danny's Balaclava* and *The Last Gardner* form part of a larger tapestry. The Right Reverend Evered appears in one story only and is never heard from again while Dod himself features in most of the tales both as the narrator and often as an active participant. Cat lovers may be perturbed at the mortality rate of the species in a couple of the stories. I make no apology for this and would remind readers that this is a work of fiction so none of the feline deaths actually occurred.

One can only imagine that Dod King intended to order these tales into an internationally famous novel at some future date but just never quite got the breaks to make it happen. So here for the first time ever in print are the collected stories of Dod King, collector of tales and one-time fictional librarian at the Invermorrisay Public Lending Library.

Enjoy.

ACKNOWLEDGEMENTS

This collection of short stories represents a departure from my previous books about the people and the places of North East Scotland. This is a work of fiction and any resemblance to any person, event or location is unintentional and purely coincidental. And it's fun writing fiction. After all, you can bump off surplus characters at random and not go to jail for murder. Or you can simply make them disappear without explanation.

I am, as always, indebted to both the oral and written recollections of the people of the North East of Scotland in the making of this book. Some of the stories were picked up in the local pubs. Others came from friends and family over the years.

Elements of *Danny's Balaclava* in chapter five were first aired as a Scratch Night play in 2015 titled *The Barber of Ferryhill*. Thanks are due to Aberdeen Lemon Tree Theatre for hosting the original idea for the story.

Special thanks are due to The Doric Board who have provided much appreciated support during the writing of this book. There's a smattering of Doric in this set of tales and if you are so minded you can read more on the interweb or listen to the likes of Scots Radio and Doric TV on your favourite podcast platform. And if the occasional word proves difficult or out of place, I can only apologise and point you to the Doric to English translations at the nether end of this book.

Thanks are also due to Grace Banks for her assistance with chapter headings and to Douglas Kynoch whose splendid Doric Dictionary proved to be an invaluable resource during the writing process.

As always, I am indebted to Paul Kohn for his little bits of guidance along the way and to Fred Wilkinson for encouraging the writing.

Duncan Harley
Inverurie 2024

SUMMER

Sunny an Weet an Micht be Het Wiks

1

A SUITCASE FULL OF MEMORIES - 4th August

George King was a local librarian fae the Aberdeenshire toon of Invermorrisay (pop 8,982 or thereabouts on Census Day 1991 and twinned with Rostov on Don). In his spare time, he penned stories about the goings on in that part of Scotland usually referred to as the North East. With the bustling fisher toons to the North and the big city of Aberdeen to the South, Invermorrisay was, and still is, slap bang in the centre of things and is well placed for a gatherer of tales.

On his days away from the library service, George would head off in search of the more unusual slices of life. The oddities and the local characters became his stock in trade and, like many a librarian before him, he dreamed of novels and fame and lucrative foreign book tours and the like. But, like many before him, he quickly found that publishers were hard to come by and that even moderate success as a writer was about as likely as lining up the lemons on a fruit machine on the hallowed eve of the Festival of St Tibbs. That said, the local papers provided some encouragement and gladly took his tales as and when it suited them which was usually when news wis short and cash wis even shorter. The editors were generally fine enough. But as George told an acquaintance at the nether end of his life, the proprietors could be difficult.

> "Sma winner yon grippy proprietors bide awa at the funcy end o toon! They'd hae the airse oot yer breeks afore they'd spend a penny on buying wirds for their skinnymalinky columns."

Known locally as Dod, which alongside being a palindrome is a North East corruption of George, he was never a language activist and only used his native Doric tongue sparingly in his reflections. Nowadays we'd maybe classify his wirds as Doric Light and I'm guessing that he wanted his stories to appeal to a wide audience. But, since he and his close kin are no longer around to ask, that's just surmise. There's also a lingering suspicion that Doric was frowned upon when he was a youngster with the lah-de-dahs in the skweels maybe thinking that Doric wis jist for feels. But truth be told, that might just be a reflection of the times when Dod was around and still kicking and folk aspired to the Queen's English.

To earn a crust, George spent most of his working life in the local library service. But he hated the job with a vengeance and all the while he was counting the days to what he hoped would be a magical and fruitful retirement. He could, after an altercation with a difficult borrower or following yet another final warning fae management, be heard muttering under his breath something like "Only another 4,873 days to go before I retire!" or "Just another 3,652 more days to go!" But it was sometimes touch and go as to whether he'd make it to that final glorious day.

Dod died shortly after retiring from the library service. He'd had a few ill things wrang wi him, so nobody was completely surprised when he went awa. He'd have retired earlier due to the ill health, but the folk in power at the local council offices kept him on in an oddly misguided attempt to care for him over the course of his various illnesses. If you dared to ask him about it, he would curse loudly and tell anybody who would listen that he'd tried desperately to keep on in his job when the Parkinsons was first flagged up all those years ago, but that "now I need out for the sake of my health, these overpaid buggers in their fancy offices want to make me suffer on till I die in these bliddy shackles."

Dod went on cursing the council bosses right up until the very end and in his more paranoid moments would tell his carers lurid tales about corruption in high places and secrets that only he could spill. But, by that time he was far gone and few folk roon aboot took much notice of his dark rantings. Such is usually the way with age when combined with infirmity.

A few years after his death, his sister Peggy moved into a care home over at Kinloch next to the cemetery where Dod lies buried and her son Airchie was tasked with emptying her house prior to selling it to fund the monthly care bills.

In the loft there was a battered suitcase full of memories. They were in the form of short stories written by Dod over the years. At first Airchie thought they were diaries. The titles included dates, but there was rarely any hint of the years these referred to. So, a tale dated August 7th sat next to January 24th. February 14th was piled on top of December 23rd and so on. There were even half written stories and, most frustrating of all, there were missing pages in amongst the scrambled mix of hand written and typed pages of the manuscript. The normally pedantic Dod, he was a librarian after all, had missed out the years and had mis-numbered some of the pages missing out crucial details such as a proper timeline. Either that, or they had been removed by him or maybe Peggy in a cover-up of some sort or other. Or, maybe he just wanted it to appear that way in order to show contempt for the normal order of things in a book of his own making. And, in a final and slightly eccentric twist, in amongst the papers in the dusty suitcase in Peggy's attic was a note in Dod's own hand listing his funeral wishes.

> It read, "No Flowers. No Psalms. No Minister. And no funeral tea. Just a decent wake and an inscription on my headstone to read 'DOD KING (MARCH 23 1929 - MARCH 23 1999 or thereabouts) NEVER KNOWINGLY MISUNDERSTOOD'."

And, if you head down to the graveyard at Kinloch, you can read this strange inscription for yourself on the family headstone right next to the big apple tree near the back gate. Only instead of Dod King it reads George King. Dod, if he were alive and kicking today, would be pure scunnered at the cheek!

2

MUSICAL BOX - 8th August

A public library, in some ways, is like a cocktail party with partygoers standing around making polite whispered conversation about Auden and Burns and the likes of Shakespeare whom everyone likes to claim to have read even when they maybe haven't taken much of it in and were forced to read it at school. If you stand around long enough, you'll meet folk who claim to have met in with Proust or Aristotle or even T.E. Lawrence in amongst the library shelves and probably some of them have actually had that experience and enjoyed every word of it.

And there was nothing especially different about the public library at Invermorrisay except that, instead of getting a complimentary glass of champagne when you first entered the place, you had to pay a pound to join. The amount would be set against the fine for any books you failed to return on time. But it was a good bargain and you might even get to meet the likes of Dod King the head librarian during your visits.

On a Wednesday in the mid-afternoon at around three-o-clock during term-time, Dod liked to hold court in the reading space at the Junior Library. It was early closing at the local academy and like as not there would be a few young regulars borrowing or returning the likes of Charlotte's Web or maybe even a Bronte book about the adventures of Jane Eyre in the romantic villages of Oakworth and Oxenhope and Stanbury or wherever. So, it was a good place to tell a tale.

But this was the Garioch in Aberdeenshire and Jane's romantic country was a thousand miles or more away from the gently swaying barley fields wrapped tight around the slopes of Ben Aucherie. So, it would have to be a guid tale about the history or the romance of the hill. Or about the great Pictish warriors or the hard-working crofter folk who once inhabited the land roon aboot.

Dod had risen to fame amongst the academy kids with his stories aboot how the spirit level had gotten its bubble and how a young lass from Drumdurno made a pact wi the deil and wis turned to a pillar o granite over at Quarthies for her trouble. The stane story wis well enough kent in the Garioch but few amongst his young audience had heard aboot how you could capture the bubbles from a lobster's fart in a glass tube and use them to measure the declination of the earth. It made him something of a hero amongst his young audience since, after all, every growing child loves a decent tale about a trouser cough especially if a nippy lobster is involved.

On this particular Wednesday there were more than a few weel kent secondary faces in the tiny library space and he gathered the dozen or so children in a broad circle at the far end of the Junior Reading Room.

As he gazed around at the youngsters, he smiled gently and said "Did I ever tell you the story about Musical Box?"

The general consensus was no. And this is more or less what he told them.

"It was about half way through The Great War you see. And folks fae a roon aboot Europe had been biding in their trenches and shooting at one another for what seemed like years. Well, it was almost four years actually. The battles had started in 1914 and by the time I'm talking about today, it was August 1918 and a lot of folks had fought and died and fought and been injured or gassed and a whole lot of other horrible things as well. There were rats as big as cats all around the trenches feasting on the rotting corpses and nobody on either side was getting anywhere fast. Despite the slaughter and all the hardships of living in amongst the filth and the blood and the mud, nobody was going anywhere at all. It was a stalemate you see. Then, along comes Musical Box to sort out the problem."

Dod paused and looked around to assess whether any of his young charges were paying attention. They all were. So, he continued.

"Now, you're maybe thinking about how a musical box wis ever going to be able to sort out a war and you'd be right to wonder. But this wis'nae ony ordinary sort of musical box. It had a big machine gun poking out at the front and anither at the back pointing ahint and two more, one at either side, as well. And the soldiers inside, and there were three of them, were sat squashed into the tiny armoured box at the back of the thing. There wis a big pair of smoky roaring engines at the front. And the tank, for that's what it was, moved around the battlefield on caterpillar tracks just like thon big bulldozer they have over at the mart for shifting coo's shites and other stinky stuff.

Now, you're maybe wondering what an army tank called Musical Box has to do wi ony o us here today. Well, there was once a young lad fae just a few miles down the road at Kinallarty and his name was Willum.

If you ever have occasion to visit Kinallarty (population 1,843 and rising) take time out to walk around the older part of the graveyard at the Northern end of the village. It's down the brae at Kinloch where auld Captain Fresson had his wee international airport that ran folk up to Orkney and just off the trunk road that leads into Invermorrisay. If you look hard enough, you'll find a gravestone in amongst the long row by the entrance with the name William Carney carved into it and a little looking up of local records informs the visitor that his date of death corresponds to the opening phase of the second Battle of Amiens in 1918. The first day of the fight to be exact. Described on the head-stone as a gunner in the Royal Tank Corps he was actually the tank's driver that fateful day and he was the son of a local farming family.

The young lad was killed in action on the eighth of August 1918, a day famously described by German General Ludendorff as 'the black day of the German army'. In August that year, British and French forces had advanced up to eleven miles Eastwards on a fifty-mile front, killing, wounding or capturing almost fifty thousand of the enemy. It was a multi-national battle. There were folk from all around the world involved in this campaign. Alongside the obligatory Americans and Canadians, the British recruited Chinese labourers to dig trenches and move supplies and build railroads.

The French, for their part, brought folk from as far away as Viet Nam and the Belgians brought in forced labourers from their various colonies over in Africa. So, there were lots of stories. But the tale of Musical Box is, I think, one of the best ones to emerge from the fighting of that summer's day. Crucially, the Germans had almost no tanks of their own and the few they had were mainly battlefield casualties captured from the British or the French. The various allies however fielded over a thousand of the things.

As I said earlier, Willum, although described as a lowly tank gunner, was in fact acting as the driver that fateful day. The three-man armoured vehicle was of a type known as a Whippet and as the name maybe suggests, it was designed to move fast and furious to exploit weaknesses in the enemy lines. These machines could reach a heady 8mph which was twice the speed of the more familiar rhomboid shaped heavy tanks usually associated with the mud and grime of trench warfare. But, like many tracked vehicles of the time, the Whippet was fiendishly difficult to drive so William Carney would have had his work cut out controlling the thing on the battlefield.

On top of that, in common with all tanks of the day, crew comfort was not a priority and a combination of fumes from both the engines and cordite smoke from the machine guns would have made life aboard quite unpleasant. And that's not even taking into account the lack of any sort of suspension and the fact that any foreigners you encountered along the way would be trying to kill you with bombs and bullets and maybe even gas. But back to Musical Box."

Dod paused for almost a minute, then opened up the book he'd been holding.

"There's a fine account of the action that day in the records of the Royal Tank Corps. It gives a blow-by-blow account of the events that led up to the death of young Willum from Kinallarty. It was based on an account recorded by the tank's commander and edited later on by a Major Wilson and headed 'The Exploits of Musical Box'. It goes something like this."

Dod began reading from the thin library bound war diary account of the exploits of the Tank Corps during that fateful August in far off 1918 on the very day when young Willum fae the tiny settlement of Kinallarty set off tae meet his maker.

"One of the most famous and bloodiest exploits by an individual tank and its crew, was done on August 8th 1918, during the first day of the Battle of Amiens - the so called "Black Day of the German Army" - when a solitary Whippet Tank, commanded by a Lieutenant Arnold, penetrated right into the rear of the German lines where it roamed around for nigh on ten hours, causing huge damage and spreading enormous confusion amongst the enemy. This is a contemporary account, based on the official records from that day."

Dod looked up from his manuscript and asked if anyone was interested in hearing more. A resounding "yes!" rang out. So, he continued the reading.

"Munchausen-like yarns have been woven out of every military campaign in history, beginning with Herodotus and continuing with Froissart and his present-day imitators. But no more unbelievable story was ever staged than that of a Whippet Tank of B Company, 6th Battalion. Other men have faced unflinchingly fearful odds to bring off forlorn hopes, but as a rule they take their adventures in sequence and at due intervals. Lieutenant Arnold, the commander of Musical Box, concentrated a whole lifetime of adventure within a single revolution of the sun. If his name had been Jack Hawkins or Horatio Nelson, one might have anticipated some buccaneering or some swashbuckling. And what Arnold did with his little machine on that fateful day was just as adventurous."

Dod had studied classics at university and, at this point in the reading he got carried away and delved somewhat deeply into ancient history. Despite this, his young audience remained attentive and dutifully munched away at the biscuits which Dod habitually provided on these occasions. He ploughed on.

"Army records generally scorn every ornamental trapping and stick closely to facts and brass tacks. They are incurably prosaic in describing even poetic happenings but, even when looked at through khaki filtered eyes, Lieutenant Arnold's assault on the German Army was not a whit less epic than the heroic defence of the Tiber bridge by Horatius in the face of overwhelming Etruscan odds in 509 BC. He was in command of Musical Box with Gunner Ribbans and Driver Carney as his crew and, against the odds, they were about to enter the history books. The trio left the lying-up point at 4.25 am (zero-hour) on 8th August 1918, and proceeded to the South side of the railway at Villers-Bretonneux. They crossed the railway line and passed through the Australian 2nd Infantry who were formed up beside some heavy Mark V. Tanks.
They then came under direct fire from a German four-gun field battery which knocked two of the slower Mark V. tanks on their flank.

On seeing this, they turned half-left and ran diagonally across the front of the enemy battery at around 600 yards range, manoeuvring so that several of their machine guns could fire all at once. They then sped round behind the Germans and attacked them from the rear. The gunners sensibly ran for their lives but gunner Ribbans finished most of them off as they retreated.

The Whippet then cruised forward and her crew shot a number of the enemy who appeared to be demoralized and unwilling to return fire. The destruction of the German battery had an immediate effect allowing the Australian infantry, who were sensibly taking cover in a sunken road, to gain ground at almost no cost in casualties.

The threesome in the Whippet then followed the railway East and came upon two cavalry patrols of twelve men each which luckily for them, they recognized as our own. They were being fired at by a party of the enemy who were hiding in the standing corn. These were quickly dealt with by machine gun fire. Going farther East, they came across a second patrol pursuing the enemy and dealt with a party of German infantrymen who had taken up a position on the railway bridge. They entered a shallow valley marked on the map as containing a German encampment and surprised a crowd of the enemy who were milling around unarmed and unaware of the presence of the whippet. Gunner Ribbans accounted for around sixty of these unfortunates in just a few minutes of firing.

The crew then set off cross country firing as they went and creating chaos behind the enemy lines. At one point they had to don respirators when the petrol tanks were penetrated by enemy bullets. But still they carried on until at about 2pm, they came upon an enemy aerodrome with a captive observation balloon dangling precariously above and a great quantity of horse-transport and motors lined up along the grass runway. Gunner Ribbans brought the balloon down with a burst of fire and stampeded the motors and transport. Then their luck ran out. Petrol was still running down the inside of the back door. As it was obvious that it was no longer possible to continue the action, Lieutenant Arnold shouted to Driver Carney to turn about, when two heavy concussions closely followed each other and the cab burst into flames. A German field gun had got in a knock-out blow.

If there ever was a situation for losing one's head it was then, the whippet crew were trapped in a burning tank, choked by smoke and petrol fumes and worn out from want of sleep and food. Carney and Ribbons got to the door and collapsed. Lieutenant Arnold was almost overcome but managed to get the door open and was able to drag out the other two. Burning petrol was running on to the ground all around the tank. When it seemed safe to do so, they all got up, and made a short rush to get away from the burning petrol. It was then that Driver Carney was shot in the stomach and killed."

Dod paused again and looked around the room expectantly. "Does anyone have a question?" he asked.

> "What happened to them after that?" asked a tiny voice from the back row.
>
> "Well," continued Dod. "It says here that Gunner Ribbans and Lieutenant Arnold somehow survived their adventure and spent the remaining weeks of the war in captivity. Mind you, their captors gave them a beating and if it hadn't been for the intervention of a German officer, things might have turned out quite differently for them. As for Willum, alongside being mentioned on the family memorial stone in Kinallarty Cemetery, he is one of those soldiers who has no known grave. But I think his name is recorded on the war memorial over at the toon centre. So, you could go and check next time you go shopping over at the square."

By this point, only around three-quarters of the youngsters remained. Some had sidled off to the sweety shop on the High Street. One had feigned a dental appointment half way through Dod's tale. Another had gone to the toilet and not returned. It was all par for the course and Dod was quite used to it. But those who remained to the bitter end seemed spellbound at the intensity of the tale. In adulthood, they would maybe, hopefully, remember that Wednesday afternoon in the children's section of the Invermorrisay Public Library when Dod King told them the tale about how young Willum from just down the road at Kinallarty drove a Musical Box into the history books at the Battle of Amiens all those years ago.

As for Dod, it was just another Wednesday and if truth be told, he didn't much like children anyway. But at least he had been spared from a dreary afternoon session on the issuing desk.

> "Roll on the weekend," he muttered quietly under his breath, "roll on the weekend!"

And he consoled himself with the thought that there were only 2,673 more such days to go before he could retire and finally get his life back.

3

A ONE-ARMED BANDIT - 14th August

Dod's great uncle George was also called Dod although some folk addressed him as Doddy. He didn't seem to mind. He had lots of stories told about him, most of which were untrue or related to the effects of drink and the adventures, both real and imagined, that the whisky might bring on. When Doddy died of natural causes though, some folk quipped that he had probably gone up in blue flames due to the effect of all that whisky and after the funeral, Dod sat down to pen a few recollections about the uncle he had heard so many tales about.

In the 1970s, nearly every toon and village in the Garioch could boast a selection of public houses and those that didn't would often have a shebeen tucked away in the back shop of the local grocer for the convenience of folk roon aboot who needed an escape from their own fireside for an hour or two of an evening. Places like Invermorrisay and Kinallarty were blessed with maybe upwards of half a dozen legal drinking houses plus a hotel or two as well. But the likes of Clacharty and Quorthies had to make do with whatever the grocer served up on his makeshift bar next to the stockroom. The rooms in these places were often spartan with wooden tea-chests for tables and whatever came to hand as seats. Sometimes there would be a fiddler rattling off a few ballads. But mostly, folk drank and played cards and maybe gossiped or complained about the weather for a few hours then trundled home to sleep it off before the early rise the next day.

Only those and those knew about these places and if you were an outsider, you would likely never get in. Old Doddy Mutch and his cronies frequented these places on a Sunday since that was the Lord's Day and you couldn't get a drink anywhere except in a hotel. And, strictly speaking, the licensing laws specified that you had to be what they called a bona-fide traveller intent on eating a substantial meal even to get that. But, for the other six days of the week he frequented the more traditional drinking establishments such as the Auld Inn at Gairnie just outside the tiny settlement that wis Pots of Clatt.

Known as Doddy to his pals but George to strangers, the old man was eventually found dead in his chair just after the start of the tattie holidays. He'd been home late the previous night and after Graeme the local taxi had dropped him off, the neighbour next door had kindly poured him in through the front door and helped him into his big arm-chair to sleep off the day's dose of medicine. It was a stroke the ended him apparently and probably in his sleep. At least that what old Doctor Morgan fae Clart reckoned, and nobody was minded to disagree. They said that the Geordie the milkie had found him when he called past to collect the arrears and for months afterwards Geordie would complain bitterly that he was still owed three weeks milk money. Eventually a neighbour of the old man, sick of all the moaning, paid the outstanding bill on behalf of the corpse just to shut the milkie up.

The news of the death was in the local paper. "Died peacefully at home" read the notice "much missed by family and Porgie." The neighbours sniggered.

Great uncle Dod was by all accounts a short dapper man with shiny brown brogues around his feet and a big pink baldie-heid tucked discreetly under his bunnet. He habitually wore a green checked sports jacket topped off with a big Grey Fergie sort of flat cap and could be seen most days tramping the two miles up the road to the inn at Gairnie at opening time, which was five-o-clock except on Sundays.

He would rarely accept a lift on the way up and local folk kent not to offer unless it was blowing an absolute hoolie or snowing hard. On the way back though, he would nearly always require a taxi and the local drivers would, often as not, have to pour him into his house then call past next day to get payment when things were clearer in the world of Doddy.

In days gone past he would travel far and wide in his search for good company. His route would usually follow mart days since folk would have money to spend and Doddy was not one to stand his hand without the prospect of a good return in kind. When the local marts began to close his travels began to decline. He was getting on in any case and several of his drinking cronies had moved on as well. One had drowned in a cattle trough up by Birtybogs after a boozy night in the grocer's back-shop, another was run down taking a shortcut over the railway out by Drinnies, a third was found tucked up behind a dyke at Pots of Clatt after the March snow melt still clutching an empty half and a half of Bells.

The publicans of the Garioch, it was rumoured, took a huge hit when Doddy Mutch finally decided to restrict his outings to the Gairnie Inn. But restrict them he did and, by the time he passed, locals had taken to referring to the place as Mutchies Bar.

Doddy's funeral was attended by around sixty folk. There were a couple of family members. A niece in her sixties came all the way from Hull and a younger brother, who lived just up the road and had given up on him years ago on account of the drinking, turned up late. There was the usual church service after which folk accompanied the man over to the graveyard for the burial.

The new minister spoke eloquently about the man. Never once mentioning the word drink, except in the context of tea and sandwiches being available over at the Gairnie Inn afterwards. He had not, he told the assembled mourners, personally had the pleasure knowing George but had chatted with someone who knew him well.

George Mutch, said The Reverend Evered, had been born just down the road at Grassick's Croft. Popular at school he became chauffeur for the local laird before joining the army at the age of eighteen, serving in France before being evacuated at Dunkirk with severe injuries including the loss of his left arm. The eulogy droned on for a further five minutes with the majority of the assembled mourners staring at the young minister in stunned silence.

Finally the churchman stopped for a wee prayer and then he orchestrated a big mournful hymn after which the coffin was gently and respectfully carried outside to the family plot to lie alongside Doddy's parents and his older sister Elsie who had died just the year before.

Almost all of the mourners turned up at the pub for the post funeral dram, eager to find out more about the Doddy they had known so little about. Amongst the buzz of conversation, comments such as "I never kent that about the man," and "So that's how he lost his arm," could be heard about the place. Doddy had of course been singularly right-handed, his empty left jacket sleeve being carefully folded and pinned up neatly at the shoulder.

It was Graeme the taxi man who finally tackled the young minister. Originally a West Coaster, he had known Doddy better than most and, alongside ferrying him about the place, had even known him briefly at secondary school. In a loud voice he complimented the minister on the service.

> "A fine service indeed Mr Evered, Doddy himself if he was de'en fine would have been most pleased, especially the bit about the big medals and all that war service. I knew the man all his life and never even knew the half of it."

> "Thank you, Mr Duff," replied the minister. "I would have been most privileged to have met Mr Mutch but as you know, I only took up my post just a week or so before his untimely death."

> "Indeed Reverend. And who was it that gave you the background information about Dod?" said Graeme the taxi.

By this point in the proceedings the drams had been downed and the wee triangular sandwiches politely chewed. There was almost complete silence as the reply came tumbling out of the minister's mouth.

"John Donald was most helpful in that respect."

"Ah right. That would be Porgie." replied Graeme.

"Why do you ask?" said the minister "and, who or what is Porgie?"

There was really no easy reply and Graeme the taxi made lame excuses then left. The next Sunday he attended the kirk for perhaps the second time since he'd met Mary. After morning service Graeme made a point of being last out in order to have a quiet word.

"Jesus, man!" he whispered loudly, "Doddy was never over at Dunkirk. In fact, he was never even a soldier. From the very day he left school, he worked at the council quarry up by Quorthies. One day, a Saturday as I recall, he got his arm caught in the crusher. It was ripped off in seconds and from what I heard he ran down the quarry brae brandishing the severed limb above his head and shouting 'Compensation! Compensation!' As for Porgie, he was Doddy's bidie-in. But we don't talk about that sort of thing much in these parts. What folks do behind closed doors is none of our affair."

And, with that he turned abruptly and strode off down the hill to the car park.

Just a few weeks later the Right Reverend Evered disappeared from view. The church authorities said that he had suffered a breakdown. But folk in these parts maybe kent better. As for Porgie? Well, he lived on for a wee bit in obscurity before slipping off in his sleep just as Doddy had done. And he ended up in the family plot alongside Doddy and Doddy's parents George and Susie and Doddy's sister Elsie. And, if truth be told, naebody fae roon aboot even batted an eyelid or thocht ony ill o it.

4

CODY'S GRAN PART ONE
GRAN CANARIA - 16th AUGUST

The McLaughlin clan were the Aberdeen branch of Dod's family on his mother's side. He'd meet up with them occasionally but mainly at weddings and funerals. When Grannie McLaughlin died in the Canaries, Dod's cousin Cody had phoned to give him the difficult news. So, he dutifully attended her funeral. When he returned home afterwards, he composed his thoughts and wrote them down in the form of a short story about how you can never really know the intimate details of the folk you thought you knew.

Cody McLaughlin was one of those lads who left the land and made a pot of money from the oil before returning to his roots. He took his big chance just at the start of the offshore boom when the government was chucking money around like it was whisky at a Highland wedding. He'd won the contract to fence off the oil terminal at Sullom Voe in the Shetlands and never looked back. He and a few mates cobbled together a work crew and got rich. They moved on to build the security fences around the big white elephant rig yard at Portivadie in Argyll and got richer. Then they went to Cromarty to repeat the exercise. After more than a decade erecting security fences, Cody came home to run a wee hobby croft and when the need arose, he'd head over to the Bank of Scotland at Invermorrisay and take out a few pounds to see him through to the next dividend pay-out on his offshore investments. And, for a while at least, he was a contented and generally happy man. That was until his schoolfriend Danny came back into his life and spilled the family beans.

The fact that Cody's gran fae Aberdeen had passed was never a huge surprise really since she had been some ripe old age or other. The real surprise was when the family learned where she had died. In the Canaries would you believe and with no travel insurance either! What to do? Return the body intact for a proper burial or lay the old woman to rest in a far-off land? Ignore the whole thing and let the authorities deal with it all? Cremate the remains and fly her back in a wee metal box? There were loads of options.

> "It's no as though she had any money set aside for all of this," moaned Cody's mum Annie. "I mean she lived on her own in a tiny wee flat in Torry. How the devil did she get there anyway? I mean the Canaries of all places! Jesus! It's a wonder they even let her on the plane. She wis steamin maist days as far as I recall. Worked part-time behind the bar at Guys on Vicky Road and never went home sober in her entire adult life. Buggered if I'm paying for this all on my own, you lot will all need to chip in tae get her back, no exceptions. Get your wallets and your purses oot!"

And chip in they did. A few thousand pounds emerged from their deep pockets plus some Euros, reluctantly in some cases though. There was even a fifty Yuan note from some distant cousin who'd been to Tibet and just wanted rid of it. Nobody noticed at the time, but Auntie Mary had quietly slipped a couple of grand into the hat. But more of this later. So, after a bit of toing and froing, Cody's gran was cremated on Gran Canaria then duly and quite expensively flown back to Aberdeen in a wee box to await the re-opening of the family lair at the Trinity and the next gathering of the clan.

Now, Trinity Cemetery lies not far from the Aberdeen beachfront and sits within sight of the creaking grandstands which are home to Aberdeen F.C. Even on a decent summers day the views are good but the breeze can be uncomfortably cold. On the day of the interment, it was wet and miserable with a big howling blaze of sticky cold sleet driving in off the North Sea with no blue skies forecast for at least a week.

There was a good turnout all considering. As well as family there were Cody's mates from Invermorrisay plus a few neighbours of old Mrs McLaughlin who in all probability had never taken much time over the old woman while she was alive but who no doubt felt obliged to show face as an indication that they maybe had looked out for her from time immemorial. Cody's sister Annie said a few words as did his brother Jesse who had flown in from Orkney especially for the occasion.

> "She was a fine woman," said Annie "always ready to help anyone and an absolute pillar of the community."
> "Aye right enough. An absolute gem. Sadly missed" shouted Jesse above the blasting wind. "Always made me scones and let me play with her budgie, before it died and went to heaven of course."

Nobody laughed. They were all too busy wiping the tears of freezing rain from their cheeks.

After a few words from the local minister, the old woman's ashes were duly lowered into the freshly opened lair and an invite went out to gather just down the road at Guys Pub for a wee libation and some of those wee triangular salmon and cucumber sandwiches and dried up sausage rolls you get at funerals throughout Scotland. All in all, there were about thirty family and friends assembled in the lounge bar seated in no particular order. Wet jackets off and pints down throat seemed the order of the day.

Cody's normally skint dad had set up a tab but no-one knew how long that would last so the race was on to down a few drinks before economic reality kicked in. The old man had worked on the rigs in the early days when men were men and oil was oil.

A big built man with an arm full of tattoos who took no prisoners, he had seemingly been impressed in his youth by the story of how Buffalo Bill Cody and his Wild West Show toured Scotland in 1904. Tales of Sioux Indians and frontiersmen battling it out on Beach Boulevard and then proceeding by train up to Banff and Fraserburgh caught his attention and he vowed to name his children after those Wild West heroes. Hence Bill Cody McLaughlin, Annie Oakley McLaughlin and following a rash drunken moment during a weekend bender, Jesse James McLaughlin emerged into the world.

Cody's mum's protestations that Jesse James was nothing but a murdering scumbag bank robber who never even featured in the Buffalo Bill tours were as nothing. She'd read all about him in the history books but Mr McLaughlin senior had a streak of the Mounties in him and he always got his way. Needless to say, Jessie and Annie had a hard time at school. Cody somehow escaped the merciless bullying and the very worst of the name calling. But that was mainly down to his big pal Danny who stood up for him when trouble brewed. That day, Danny was seated three tables down from the bar still wearing the brown knitted weatherproof balaclava which he had worn throughout the graveside proceedings.

Cody sidled over and sat down beside his friend. "How you doing pal? Fine you could come. Gran would have liked that."

Danny grunted a muffled reply then turned to Cody's Auntie Mary, "sorry for your loss Mary, she was well respected. Sad loss indeed!"

Mary, glass in hand, turned round to face him. "Cheers, she was a bit dottered by the end but there but for the grace etc. How are you doing? Been a while."

"Great," replied the balaclava'd Danny. "Working here and there, mainly offshore doing this and that. So, canny complain really. Even if I did, no-one would take any notice. All good, all good really, honest injuns. Nice to see you again Mary."

More small talk and platitudes followed and Mary either never noticed or never let on that she had clocked the brown knitted balaclava. By this time, the drink had kicked in and folk around the bar were rattling on and on about how granny was such a lovely woman, always there when you needed help. How, they don't make them like her nowadays! And how she'd had such a long and fruitful life. Oddly, nobody mentioned the Canaries again. Until that is, a muffled voice was heard from table three. It was Danny.

"How come she was buried in the Trinity? And how come she ended up in the Canaries?"

"Fit wis that you said Danny?" said Mary, turning in her seat to stare at him.

"How come she was buried in the Trinity ah said? She made a point of never visiting the place. Said it wis haunted or something. Told me it was bad luck to take the short cut through the graveyard down to the beach. Scared the life out of us kids." came the reply.

The balaclava'd Danny had spoken. A big silence followed, broken only when Auntie Mary began to sniffle. After maybe a full thirty seconds she dabbed at her mascara, recovered some composure and began to tell a tale.

"Well, when I was in primary, we lived in King Street just down from the old fire station. Our mum would often take us down the beach after school. We used to take a short cut through the cemetery. There's a path down past Urquhart Road to Park Road if you know. I don't really remember exactly when it was, but one day we were halfway down and we heard a loud throbbing noise up above. I was too young to take much heed but your gran knew what it was.

'Run, get doon behind that stane,' she shouted as a big blue aeroplane roared overhead from the sea.

We stared as it passed over and I can still remember the aircraft gunner looking down at us as we lay flat on the ground. You can still see the bullet holes in the gravestone where he missed us. Our mum refused to let us go there after that. Suppose that's when Mary took to frightening me about how it was haunted by ghoulies and the like, just to keep me safe. As for why she's buried there, it's the family plot Danny. Where else wid we put her?"

No one spoke for a bit. Then the drink kicked in again and folk began to tell jokes about the Hitler war, about football heroes and about some hairbrained cooncil scheme to build a car park in Union Terrace Gardens.

Cody turned to Danny. "Why the balaclava?"

Slowly, ever so slowly, Danny pulled off his headgear to reveal a big patch of bright red forehead and a headful of singed hair and a missing eyebrow.

"It's a long story. I'll maybe enlighten you in private a bit later." said the virtually hairless Danny.

5

CODY'S GRAN PART TWO
DANNY'S BALACLAVA - 16th August

After the funeral lunch, Cody and Danny headed off into toon. Guys Pub, where the family gathering had been, was closing for the rest of the afternoon and the pair bused it down to Belmont Street for more libation and a chance to catch up in private. The tab at Guys had run out anyway and the prospect of big rounds held little appeal. So, the pair said their goodbyes and shook a few hands and left the few remaining mourners to do whatever folk do after a funeral lunch. Señora McLaughlin had had her final goodbye and that was that as far as Cody was concerned. Or so he thought. Fresh pints in hand they chose a secluded window seat in the basement of The Frog and Kilt.

It was Cody who spoke first. "So, why the Balaclava Danny?"

Danny thought for a minute. They'd hardly spoken on the bus and he'd hoped the topic had been forgotten about. But, obviously not.

"It's a long story," he replied. "A really long story."
"Well, go on, do tell." said Cody.
Wrong question thought Danny and burst out with a mock affrontit
"Christ, is that all you want to know?" I mean, for God's sake, can't a man wear a wee disguise if he wants to? I mean, what's the problem? It's no as if I'm a liquor store bandit or anything."

Now, you'd have had to be blind not to notice Danny's disguise. A hoody is one thing but a balaclava is quite something else. Facial recognition was quite out of the question but as a disguise it was a complete disaster. It was August after all, and unless you were heading out into the wilds of the North Sea or up some Munro or other, there was absolutely no reason to wear a balaclava, unless you were indeed about to rob a bank or a post office. Try a different tack thought Cody.

"If you'd rather not say too much, that's absolutely fine. At the risk of repetition, what's your pleasure? Today, in addition to some foaming wort, we have on offer some white. We have on offer, a few small bags of an off-white dolly mixture plus some other more euphoric colours should Sir require. This stuff may blow your mind big time, all rights reserved of course and should Sir feel unwell afterwards, we urgently advise the calling of GDOC's or similar. All rights reserved of course yet again. Care to partake? Of course, we completely understand if Sir declines this once only offer!"

Danny took the hint and after a wee snort in the toilets, he relaxed and began to open up.

"Ah had some business with some associates of your gran in Peterhead a year or so back. And see all that pillar of the community stuff, the 'She was a fine woman' and all that. Aye, shite!"

He paused to wipe some powder off his nose.

"She was a bit of a drug courier is what ah heard. Just when she needed extra money you understand. She worked for some shady toffs from over in Mannofield who sent her abroad for the occasional holiday and used her to take out the cash to pay their import bills.

She never touched the drugs though. Just the cash. Big bundles stuffed into her suitcase. Maybe once a month for a while. That's why she was in Gran Canaria. It certainly wisnae for the benefit of her health. It paid the rent. Been doing it for years. After all who'd search an old wrinkled grannie on her way back frae her holiday in the sun. Word was they'd paid off the customs fowk as well, just for some extra insurance so she was never caught and never ended up in the jail."

By now he had Cody's full attention.

"So, I mean, how do you know all this Danny? And how come I never had even a wee snifter aboot any of it? You'll be telling me next that Grannie McGlaughlin introduced the chanter to her native Scotland next! Or maybe she invented polar bears! Fit fuckin planet are ye on man? A mean, get real for goodness-sake!"

Now it turned out that, a year or so back amongst the shards of history, Danny's long time school pal McAllister had retired from the police. At the rank of Inspector, McAllister had done well. Not only that, but he'd kept his hands squeaky clean throughout his time in the force. No unfortunate incidents in the cells and no hint of misconduct had marred his unblemished career. As a result, it was really no surprise when he received a phone call from an ex-colleague just a month or so after the retiral party. Would he be interested in some part time work up in Peterhead? Just a little matter of surveillance you understand, nothing strenuous. Absolutely no personal risk involved. Payment in cash plus expenses. Transport supplied. Just a couple of days a week. Easy money. It sounded almost too good to be true. But in no time at all McAllister found himself back on the force as an unofficial contractor to HM Customs and

Excise and with a brief to recruit a colleague to assist in the surveillance operation. He phoned Danny and in no time at all they teamed up and tooled up for what promised to be easy money.

The couple of days a week turned into a couple of nights a week, sitting in an old van on the quayside at Fraserburgh and sometimes Peterhead. The little matter of surveillance involved monitoring the harbour area and dockside bars for unusual activity involving the supply of class A substances. The "easy money" bit was true enough though, at least for a while.

So that was how Danny got involved in the drug business. The training duly took place over a couple of weekends. How to take detailed notes using a voice recorder. What type of vehicle to use. Vans are best, no-one will notice you and you can observe from the back without being seen. When shooting video create definite borders between clips by placing hand over camera at the end of each segment. Make sure that a time and date stamp appears on the footage. Always obtain a panoramic video shot of the location and record images of any persons or vehicles for use as verification that the person being observed was there.

Don't do surveillance by yourself. It isn't a single-person activity and keep a plastic bag, a roll of toilet paper and an empty plastic bottle in your vehicle at all times. Stakeouts can last for hours. There was a talk on passive self-defence by a psychologist and a retired Irish police inspector delivered a lecture on the defusing of potentially violent situations which concluded with some helpful advice.

"If in any doubt about your personal safety, the best thing to do is leg it as fast as you can." So began Danny's new undercover career.

The first few weeks were uninvitingly boring but profitable. The pay cheques rolled in but nothing much happened. Two nights a week Danny and McAllister picked up a van from the Custom House car park in Guild Street and drove to various North East ports. The first job involved the small tightly packed marina at Findochty. Situated some four miles from Buckie and on the shores of the Moray Firth, a more unlikely location for the smuggling of drugs could in all probability not be imagined. A one pub toon, Findochty boasts a population of eleven hundred souls who attend six churches including those of the Plymouth

Brethren and the Salvation Army. The place was deserted at most times of day but boasted curtain twitchers peering out from behind lounge windows looking out at anything which moved. In truth, the excise men would have been better enlisting the locals for the surveillance instead of the two men in the rusty red van. A weekend's surveillance in glorious Buckie followed, again with nothing to report. Then came Fraserburgh.

Operation Moravia, a nationwide drugs operation, had just concluded with some arrests in Dufftown and Elgin. McAllister had been asked to look out for new blood moving into the newly vacant territory to fill the vacuum left by the arrests. Men who looked out of place, expensive vehicles parked outside clubs and pubs late at night. Men in suits carrying bulky shoulder bags, foreign boats, suspicious characters, suspicious behaviour. In short anything unusual in a busy North East harbour toon.

The first few nights were fairly uneventful. A few drunks, a few minor fights and the usual harbourside comings and goings. Nothing much to report and nothing much to film. The standing instructions were to record number plates for later analysis and, if possible, take photos of all vehicles in the harbour area. Facial shots of drivers and passengers were also required providing this could be done unobserved from inside the van. On no account were either of the men to leave the vehicle and if compromised in any way, they were to drive off and avoid any potential confrontation.

It had been a long night and Danny had just about drifted off when he heard McAllister's camera whirring.

"What's up?" he mumbled.
"There's that car again" came the reply. "Third time it's been round past. Red BMW, two guys in front, might be one in back. Can't be sure though."
Got it," said Danny "what do you think?"
"Odd, slowing down just opposite then off again. Maybe just youngsters out partying. Get a still photo if it comes round again," said McAllister.

A few minutes later the red BMW appeared again. This time it stopped maybe twenty yards away from the front of the van with its lights on full beam. Three hoodied men got out slowly and, as if in no particular hurry, walked leisurely up to the front of the van. Both Danny and McAllister realised that one appeared to be carrying a small axe. As the pair watched in disbelief, the man swung the axe and the driver's side window disintegrated in a shower of splinters allowing a blast of cold damp November air to flood the interior of the van. The second figure pulled out a small yellow canister and the unmistakable smell of lighter fluid filled the confined space.

"Must be freezing in that van pal," said the man with the yellow can. "Here's a wee present from the Broch to heat you up a bit. Next time we see you around here, you might end up in the harbour. Take a wee hint and fuck right off back where you came from."

With that, he produced a cigarette lighter and lit the stream of liquid that was still spraying from the wee yellow can. There was a soft whooshing sound accompanied by a bluish flame and then a blast of heat swept through the van.

"Jesus, get the fuck oot," shouted McAllister.

Danny hurled himself at the now partially open back doors where McAllister, having seen what was coming, was standing with a jacket in front of his face shouting something unintelligible. The sulphurous stench of burnt hair filled Danny's nostrils. He hadn't smelt that since the day his cat caught fire in front of the electric heater a few winters ago. He picked himself up and looked around only to find McAllister standing laughing at him.

"What's the joke?" he spluttered. "Have they gone? What's so funny?"

"Your hairs all burnt off on the one side and you've only got half an eyebrow left," came the reply. "Aye, they've gone, it was just a friendly warning."

Danny stared at him in disbelief. "Friendly? Could have killed us both if you ask me! Get me oot o here fast before they come back after us again!"

With that, Danny's promising but short career as an undercover investigator came to a fiery end. He collected his cash for the job and hid in his flat for a week hoping that the missing hair would grow back in. Each day, he checked the mirror for signs of regeneration. Each night, he applied hair tonic bought for him by a sympathetic neighbour.

On the Friday following the Fraserburgh episode, Danny's phone rang. It was Cody's sister Annie calling to inform him about Granny McGlaughlin's demise. Could he come to the funeral? Now, Danny had always had a soft spot for Annie. Just friends, platonic you understand. But good friends. He told her about his predicament, about how half of his head resembled a burnt mattress, about his missing eyebrow, about the hair tonic.

Cody rocked with laughter, "so what did she say?"

"At first," said Danny "she just laughed, guess she didn't believe me. Then she came round for a look and laughed some more. Said it might take months to grow back in and that I couldn't hide in the flat forever. Suggested the balaclava idea. After all, who would think it odd. Need to wrap up warm and all that. Worked a treat didn't it!"

"Ah right" replied Cody. "Well good for you, well done. Must have taken a lot of courage to walk into Guys with that thing on your head."

Another round was duly ordered plus some crisps and a couple of cheese toasties. The two funeral refugees munched in silence. Then all of a sudden, Cody remembered Danny's talk about his gran being a drug courier.

"What made you say my grannie was a mule, Danny?"

Danny looked thoughtful for a minute then, having decided that it was maybe a good time to reveal all, he looked Cody straight in the eyes.

"Well, as I said, she'd being doing it for years. Surely you must have known pal. That wee room and kitchen flat in Torry was just a front. Your Auntie Mary was in on it as well and between the pair of them they must have earned enough to buy half of the tenements on Albert Road at one time. God only knows why she went back for one final run. Maybe it was the better weather or something. She certainly didn't need the money!"

Cody made a mental note to have a serious word with Mary later on in the week.

6

CODY'S GRAN PART THREE
MARY - 19th August

Cody planned to meet up with Mary the following Saturday for a lunchtime pint at Guys. It had been a busy week what with the funeral and all. But the questions surrounding Grannie McGlaughlin's secret life kept bouncing around his head and keeping him awake at night. So, he gritted his teeth and made the call.

"Fancy a liquid lunch on Saturday at Guys Mary? I'm paying. Have anything you want and we can have a pie and chips as well. Be fine to have a proper catch up."

The bar was heaving when they arrived so they headed off to the snug. It was match-day and the place was full of punters throwing back a few before kick-off. They'd mostly be back a couple of hours later to celebrate or commiserate before making an unsteady way home after dark with a chip shop stop and maybe a pause to water a few gardens along the way. But the snug was empty and, after ordering, they settled down beside the hearth to warm up and dry out.

It was Mary who spoke first. "Heard you wanted to find oot mair about Grannie's foreign holidays. And, before you get uppity, it was Danny what told me. He said he felt obliged to warn me so I could work up a cover story. But I've decided to spill the beans as it were. Give you the full story. After all, what harm could it do now she's died?"

Cody was quite taken aback. He'd expected a few minutes of denial at the very least, and here was Mary offering to blurt it all out without even a struggle.

"Aye, fine Mary. Am all ears. Let's hear it then!"

Now, as far as Cody was concerned, Mary had had a difficult life. An underdog if there was indeed such a thing, she had married young and suffered for it. Her first husband Michael had been a gambler and Mary's family had never really come to terms with that. Then the beatings started and the family looked the other way and left her alone to deal with the situation. After the children arrived, she kept her hand firmly on her purse and bided her time and planned for what she hoped would be a better future once they were all grown up.

"I'll bide with the bastard till they're out of school," she told a friend. "Then I'm off awa! No question about it!"

A few years later she told another friend that she'd maybe bide a bit longer until the two lads had landed decent jobs or maybe even done university. After a few more years, she realised that life with Michael was never going to change so she left him for another man. But that was only short term. The other man was just as hopeless and beat her as well. It was a well-worn story and an eggshell path hard for a woman to navigate. But escape she did. But not in the way that Cody was expecting.

What followed was astonishing. The food arrived and over the next hour along with some drinks, Mary told a story the like of which he never could have begun to imagine. Seems Mary and Grannie McLaughlin had been partners on the fringes of the drugs trade since he'd been a wee boy. And, until the funeral, they'd managed to keep it all fairly secret.

"It was never the plan you understand. I mean, I'd partied a bit like you do when you're young and I'd tried a few illicit substances on rare occasions. But I'd never imagined for a minute I'd ever be involved in shipping the stuff in from abroad. I mean you wouldn't, would you? Looking back, it was easy money once you got used to the routine and the risks. Plus, we never got caught, unless you count the taxing by the local gangs. Then there were all the pay offs for the polis and the customs and that could be expensive. But it was the stripping that started it all off really."

Cody stared at her wide eyed. "The stripping?"

"Aye, the stripping. And the escort agency, although that was never really a big part of the business. Oh, and the money lending. Although that came later before the drug money got into full swing."

"I'm all ears." replied the stunned Cody.

Turned out that Mary and her first ex and then her second ex had been running strippers all around the North East. The business grew and grew and the profits flowed in. Pubs and clubs couldn't get enough and then there were the private parties in the backrooms of the country hotels. Staggers and Hens and the like. Plus, the odd wedding. There was even a booking for a wake.

The more private, the better the money. There seemed no end to it. And then the big boys moved in. Paddy, Mary's violent second ex, had ended up in Craiginches for a spell and the pressure was on to hand over the business in exchange for immunity from the law or more likely immunity from a painful beating or a stabbing in the jail.

Mary went to Grannie McLaughlin for advice and for a time the two women held off the takeover bids until the pressure proved too much. Paddy got himself killed in prison and Michael, her first man, had ended up in a Spanish gaol after a tip off from a rival smuggling gang. Word was Paddy had accidentally fallen off a prison balcony and word was that Mary would likely be next to suffer an accident. It was time to cave in.

"There was some room for negotiation." said Mary. "They let us keep the money lending part of the business providing we only lent out in Torry. But eventually they took that off us as well. They were only waiting to see how it worked really. Then they taxed us out of business. And in the end, we were left with just a few dozen suitcases full of squirreled cash. That was how we bought all the flats you see."

"The flats?" said Cody. "I thought Grannie McGlaughlin was skint"

"No, no, not at all!" replied Mary. "She was never skint. But to keep up appearances we had to make it look as though she was. Otherwise, those bastards would have made a move on the rental business as well. That was why she made the Spanish trips. Oh, she did smuggle the money abroad for the drug folk right enough. But it was just a front. I mean, she owned half of Albert Road. Neither of us needed money but, we couldn't let on if you understand."

She paused for a minute before continuing.

"It's all owned through front companies otherwise they'd have moved on us and taken it all away in an instant. And come to think of it, so would the Revenue if they ever got wind of where it all came fae. You learn from past mistakes after all. And don't worry, it's all legit now and when I go, you and the rest of the family will get the lot no questions asked. The fancy lawyers and the dodgy accountants have sorted it all out. You'll maybe not have to do a day's dishonest work again after I'm gone Cody. Providing that is, you can keep a secret! So maybe think on that before you go telling on me to anyone. Look to the future and maybe don't ask any more about where it all came from. There's no point rocking the boat after the storm has passed after all."

A few pleasantries later, the still stunned Cody dutifully got up to pay the bill for lunch. As prepared to head to the bar, he heard Mary whisper softly.

> "And you'll not be doing that either. Put that wallet away. Now that Granny's gone, I own Guys and, for that matter, I own half of Torry as weel and I'll not have any of my kith and kin forking out a penny in the place. So, sit ye doon laddie an jist dee as yer telt. Just act as if you own the place. And you will come time!"

Cody did exactly as he was told. After all, Mary was family and now that he was heir to the place he wasn't about to complain.

A few years later, Mary decided to retire to the Bahamas with the new love of her life, a St Bernard called Bessie. Before she left for abroad, she summoned Bill Cody and Annie Oakley and Jesse James to a meeting with her fancy lawyers in Carden Place. There, in front of legal witnesses, she signed over Guys to the threesome for a nominal pound and threw in a dozen of her rental flats as well as a sweetener.

The only condition of the gift was that when the time came, the three of them would arrange to have her body cremated then sent back to Aberdeen to be interred beside Grannie McGlaughlin in the family lair at The Trinity. To seal that part of the deal, on the way out, she handed Cody a big brown envelope full of cash for that final ticket home. When Cody protested that she'd already given them more than enough she stopped and smiled.

> "jist dee as yer telt laddie. Put that in the safe for when its needed. And mind and feed the pub cat her favourite chicken denner."

And that, for what it's worth, is how a bunch of cowboys rose to prominence as undercover millionaires in Torry.

7

AIRCHIE'S WINDMILL – 22nd August

To say that Airchie van Dijk's vintage Morris Minor motor car was a horrible machine would probably be an understatement. When it went, which was just occasionally, it rattled and rolled on corners and backfired whenever you changed gear. In the rain, if it went at all, the boot filled up with water and the wipers, when they worked, never went quite fast enough to make a difference at speeds above thirty miles an hour.

It was one of those split windscreen export jobs from the early 1950s with all the usual faults and a bad paint job to boot. Word was that in those days most of the Morris factory cars went for export to pay off the war debt and Florence, for that was her name, was one of these. Left hand drive and riddled with rust, she'd made it back to her native country when Airchie's mother-in-law Beatrix had bought the croft at Glachan on the narrow track up to the car park at the Back of Ben Aucherie. Amazingly, Florence survived the trip across the Channel and up to Aberdeenshire and during Beatrix's brief stay at Glachan she could often be seen rattling around the countryside trailing a plume of blue smoke. Eventually though she simply refused to start and was unceremoniously manhandled into the field behind the hen shed to await her maker.

Beatrix had moved to the Garioch for a new start. She'd met a fine enough looking lad from Invermorrisay in her native Amsterdam and the pair soon made the tiny croft house habitable with what was left of her money from the cannabis trade. She'd part-owned a coffee shop in De Wallen and sold her interest in the enterprise to fund her new life in Scotland but, as is often the case with major lifestyle changes, it had never quite worked out as expected. The boyfriend walked out on her within a few months of their arrival in Aberdeenshire and Beatrix found herself alone and homesick in a foreign land. She soon moved back to Holland and bought her way back into the De Wallen red-light district selling coffee and legal highs to the cannabis tourists on Koestraat and she never visited mainland Scotland ever again.

The croft lay empty for a couple of years until Beatrix's daughter Frederica and her man Airchie decided to give crofting a go. Frederica was a language teacher and soon got herself a job at the local academy. Airchie on the other hand was a long-haired hippie who had a predilection for acid and cocaine.

Now, Airchie wisna van Dijk's real name. That was just what the folks round about called him since Boudewijn, his given name, didn't exactly roll off the tongue. So Airchie it was and Boudewijn didn't really seem to mind that much. In fact, he took it as a sign that he was now accepted as one of the locals.

Dod had met in with Airchie at the library a couple of years previously and the pair had hit it off. The big Dutchman had a decent sense of humour and that appealed to Dod. So, he soon had a standing invitation to call by the Dutchman's tiny croft if he was ever on his way past on his way up or back down the Hill of Ben Aucherie which wasn't as often as he would have liked.

The croft had seen better days when Frederica and Airchie arrived to take it over. The weather had played havoc with the place during the two years it lay empty and the mice had moved in. In much earlier times it would have sported a kailyard and maybe a milk cow or two along with some grunters as well as the obligatory hens and deuks. But time and the Amsterdam money had changed the need for all of that and it wasn't long before the Dutch folk had transformed what was by then a tummle-doon wreck of a place into something more suited to genteel Twentieth Century country living. The ancient lath and plaster walls were stripped back to the stone then rebuilt with modern plasterboard. A damp course was dug to stop the water getting in from below and a new roof was erected to stop it getting in from above. The two tiny out-fields became one big vegetable garden and the ancient outhouses were demolished to make way for the chalet which was originally planned to house Beatrix should she ever return. But she never did return and if asked why, would cite clegs and midges and that biting cold winter wind as the reason despite everyone knowing that it was in reality down to broken dreams.

All the while the renovations were happening, Florence the Morris Minor sat abandoned and derelict in the corner of the field behind the old hen shed. In summer she was hidden behind a green wall of docks and nettles. In the depths of winter, the snow hid all the rust and made her look quite appealing. And in the spring after the chalet was built, Airchie got her going again. She'd never have passed the MOT test. But for the price of a fresh set of spark plugs and a few hours tinkering with a spanner she started up and went back on the road for a bit.

It wasn't long before she broke down again though, and this time it was terminal. The suspension had collapsed overnight and even the most dedicated owner would have seen the light and phoned the local scrappy. But not Airchie. He'd been reading up about windmills. And so it was that Florence the Morris Minor was transformed into the very first wind-turbine to be erected on the slopes of Ben Aucherie.

It wasn't as if Airchie and his lady really needed an off-grid power supply. Apart from an occasional power cut in winter, the Hydro Electric Board supply that ran by the croft was more than adequate. And if truth be told, an occasional blackout provided a welcome reason to break out the paraffin lamp and light up the open fire in the lounge for a romantic evening. But they'd been reading one of those Mother Earth back to basics lifestyle compendiums and the notion of free power had gotten Airchie all fired up and raring to prove that, come the apocalypse, they would survive no matter what the complete collapse of Western civilisation, as we know it, threw at them.

Over the course of a few weeks he raided Florence for parts. The boot lid and some slices of the bonnet were cut up to make the turbine blades which were bolted onto the vehicle's cooling fan then attached by a series of fan-belts and pulleys to the alternator. The voltage regulator was wired in using parts of Florence's wiring loom and a chain from an old bicycle linked the main fan assembly to what had at one time been the offside brake assembly of the deceased Mk1 Morris Minor as an emergency brake. Finally, the whole shebang was bolted onto a gigantic chrome plated bracket formed from the vehicles rear bumper and then attached to a steel frame made from laminated sections of what remained of Florence's rusting roof. It was by no means a pretty looking machine but Airchie was confident that his creation would produce the goods.

> "I reckon it should produce enough electricity to power a few lights and maybe even the TV in the house and maybe charge up a couple of six-volt car batteries as storage as well," he would tell folk. "I'm thinking maybe 14.3 volts DC at 12 amperes or thereabouts when the wind is right and as much as 9.7 volts at 8.6 amperes on a calmer day."

He would then produce a sheaf of complicated A-4 calculations to prove his point. It all looked terribly technical.

No one from round about was minded to challenge his calculations since no one could even begin to understand them and, in due course, an old GPO telegraph pole was purchased from a neighbouring farmer to mount the whole contraption on to.

> "That bloody pole cost more than the entire turbine took to make," moaned Airchie to anyone who would listen. And, in a final flourish, he mounted one of Florence's tail lamps on the top of the mast.
> "You can't be too careful," he told his wife. "There's just a chance of a low flying helicopter coming this way. Better I think, to be safe than sorry! We don't want any accidents after all."

The prophetic nature of his words would soon become clear, but not because of helicopters.

On the appointed day of the inauguration of the new machine, a clutch of curious neighbours turned up along with a dozen or so local alternative types who had heard on the grapevine that along with unveiling of the new windmill, there was a decent chance that Beatrix, although unlikely to be there in person, might have sent over some of her famous chocolate and cherry cake all the way from the back streets of Amsterdam.

All in all, there must have been, if you count the children, around forty folk traipsing aboot the Dutchman's back garden on the big day. The hens and the deuks had been shut in specially in for the occasion and Ethel, the van Dijk's solitary sow, was screeching and grunting around the place as if unsure about the invasion of her home territory by this bunch of strangers.

Then there was Angus. He'd been saved from the slaughterhouse when Beatrix had moved in and had been looked after by a neighbour for a bit before moving back to the outfield when Airchie and Frederica took possession of the place. Unphased by all the commotion, he just kept on munching the grass whilst keeping a wary eye on all the food that was being trotted out. He was maybe just waiting his chance for a fancy bit. For that's what goats do. As for the cats, they were keeping well out of the way and observed the proceedings from high up in the branches of the big ash tree beside the croft house.

A deep but narrow hole had been prepared to house the base of the telegraph pole and there were stay wires already set into the ground on three sides. All that remained was to drop the pole into the ground, attach the stays and infill the hole. The cabling to the house was already in place and, according to Airchie, it would be a matter of minutes to make the final connections once the turbine was up and running.

Along with the potlucks and the wine that folk had brought, there was pizza and soft drinks for the kids and the chalet kitchen was set up as a help-yourself bar with a barrel of beer and some flagons of cider on tap for the adults. And there was a rumour that there was indeed likely to be cake. But only towards midnight when the families had gone home and the throng of turbine engineers had thinned out a bit.

The main event was scheduled for 2pm but with rain and gusts of wind threatening, Airchie was persuaded to delay the erection of the pole and the home-made turbine for a bit to see if the wind would die down and by half-past three conditions were looking more promising. By this time of the day, Airchie and his erection team had been drinking for several hours and were brim full of enthusiasm. A rebuke from Frederica came to nothing and in the late afternoon the inebriated lads began the task of lowering the base of the pole into the ground.

Things appeared to go smoothly. Several of the helpers held the structure plumb while the base was infilled with stones and earth. A mix of concrete was prepared then poured in to set and finally the three wire stays were secured to the ground then tensioned to keep the structure stable while the concrete set. Airchie had reckoned that it would take around twenty-four hours to cure sufficiently for the turbine to be tested and as he stood back to admire his creation, he announced that all and sundry were invited back the very next day to witness the grand start-up of the device.

After more pizza and more cider, folk began to drift off home and by around 8pm only a few stalwarts were left. As darkness descended, a log fire was lit in the firepit near the foot of the turbine and Airchie headed indoors reappearing a few minutes later with a large round metal biscuit tin which contained the cake that Beatrix had posted from Amsterdam. There was an excited buzz of interest around the camp fire and the ten or so folk who had stayed for the real main event watched expectantly as Airchie produced a large kitchen knife and began slowly and deliberately slicing up the chocolate and cherry cake on the serving table alongside the pizza oven.

First, he cut the cake precisely in half and put half back into the tin. Then he cut the remaining half in half and placed the quarter in the tin beside the half. Then, to the consternation of those present, he halved the remaining quarter and placed half of that portion in the tin beside the rest. The portion that remained on the table looked tiny compared to the original whole cake but then Airchie began to half that again then he halved the halves until after several more operations he had exactly sixteen wafer thin slices of cake in front of him along with a very few crumbs which he carefully gathered up and put back in the tin beside the larger portions of the cake.

"Is that all we're getting then?" chorused the group.

"It's all you'll likely be needing and more!" came Airchie's reply. "And you'd be well advised not to wander off once you've had your slice of cake. There's likely to be Tralfamadorians about on the hill tonight, or so it goes."

The plate with the carefully measured out slices of cake was passed from hand to hand around the fire and each turbine engineer in turn carefully consumed his allotted piece amidst a general chatter. Then one by one, the participants became silent and all that could be heard was the crackling of the logs on the fire and the rustling of the leaves on the big ash tree beside the house. Nobody moved much and all eyes were on the fire in contemplative silence as the main ingredient of the cake took effect.

For his part, Dod had never dabbled in drugs in his entire life and although he had some idea that the cake was laced with an illicit substance, the fact that it had arrived unopened and intact via the British postal system seemed somehow to allay any last-minute reservations he might have had. And, it was after all just a tiny piece of chocolate cake. What could possibly be the harm in it?

The rush took him by surprise. One minute he was lusting after an extra slice of Beatrix's delicious chocolate cake. The next he was wishing he had gone home earlier and was inwardly swearing to his maker never to succumb to chocolate cake ever again. He felt his body slowly melt into the ground and try as he might, he found that he couldn't move his arms or his legs. He tried to speak but nothing came out. His tongue was numb and his lips felt as if they were made of rubber. Then the Tralfamadorians appeared.

At first, they just circled the campfire in complete silence. Then, as time passed, they stopped and looked directly at him. They looked just as Billy Pilgrim had described them. Four-dimensional and green and toilet plunger shaped, they resembled a hand with an eye in the centre. He wasn't at all afraid of them. Just resigned and fascinated by it all. Maybe he would end up being transported to a zoo. That had never happened to him before. Maybe he would learn how to commune with the other animals. That had never happened either. He wondered if he would be allowed to keep his clothes and what sort of food he might be given. There were so many unknowns.

After a while, the Tralfamadorians began to chant in unison. At first, he couldn't make it out. But then the words became clear.

"All moments, past, present, and future, always have existed, always will exist. All moments, past, present, and future, always have existed, always will exist. All moments, past, present, and future, always have existed, always will exist."

That was it. This was answer he had been looking for all of his life. He tried to reach into his pocket for a pen to write it all down. But he still couldn't move his arms and his fingers felt completely numb. In a panic he looked around hoping that someone beside him had heard the chant. But he soon realised that they were in a different space and that the words had been given to him and him alone as a gift from another dimension.

He began inwardly repeating the chant. That would do it. Once things returned to normal, once the effects of the chocolate cake from Amsterdam wore off, the mantra would be indelibly etched in his mind! He had been given the answer to the ultimate mystery of the universe and he wasn't about to forget it!

As the fire died down, the wind got up and the Tralfamadorians gradually disappeared from view. They sort of faded into the shadows although Dod, who was the only one who'd actually seen them, was aware that they were still lurking. It was just that you couldn't see them no matter how hard you looked. But they were still watching from the shadows and listening to his thoughts to see if he had understood the wisdom they had shared. Somehow it all made sense to him. How could it not?

Someone passed round a bottle of mineral water and those stalwarts who were still awake began to emerge from their cake induced trance. Nobody spoke much. But it was obvious that the drug in the cake, whatever it was, was fast wearing off.

By around 2.30am, the moon had risen and in the chill of the night a few individuals had sloped off to the croft house to catch a bit of sleep before dawn. A couple of the revellers had headed down to the outfield to get a better view of the stars and that was when Angus got out through the open gate.

Angus, like so many of his kind, would eat almost anything. When he got fed up with a diet of thistles and nettles, he would raid the washing line for socks to eat and underpants to chew on and if you left the kitchen door ajar, he'd likely be found in amongst the dirty laundry with a mouthful of cat food or someone's knickers between his jaws. It wasn't that he was unruly, just that he was by nature an opportunist. So, when Angus stumbled across the remains of someone's slice of chocolate cake he didn't hesitate for a moment. In truth it was just a few crumbs and a piece of discarded cherry. A human would have been hard put to feel any effect from the abandoned cake. But for a goat, the effect was electrifying.

The first anyone knew of the goats escape was when a loud grinding noise was heard from the direction of the windmill. This was accompanied by a few blue and orange sparks and before anyone could react a small fire had erupted from the gearbox mechanism perched on top of the turbine pole. As they watched in utter disbelief, Angus could be seen stumbling madly round and round the base of the pole in ever decreasing circles with the electrical distribution cables wrapped loosely around his hind legs. In his mouth were the partially chewed remnants of the hemp rope that had secured the brake mechanism for the turbine and, in his eyes, there was what Dod would later recall as a look of wild terror as the now blazing windmill lit up the entire garden like a giant November sparkler.

Eventually the drug fuelled Angus ran out of room to manoeuvre as the cable wrapped more and more tightly around the base of the telegraph pole and with a mighty lunge, he broke free and without looking either right or left, trotted unsteadily through the gate and back into his field to bed down in his shelter for the remainder of the night.

Finally, and with the Easterly wind now getting up and the home made turbine blades spinning completely out of control, the fresh concrete at the base of the pole began to break apart and the machine at the top of the pole began to topple slowly towards the house its fall broken only by the overhead Hydro line which brought in the electricity supply from the National Grid. There was a small explosion and, with a blinding flash which lit up the entire hillside, every house within a mile of the croft was blacked out for the remainder of the day.

When the engineers from the Hydro Board investigated, the whole episode was written off as an unfortunate accident. But everyone who witnessed the turbine disaster, including Dod, knew better. Some put it down to the cake from Amsterdam. Some blamed the goat. Someone in the group even blamed poor Florence. As for Dod, he was inclined to place the blame squarely on the

Tralfamadorians.

The day after the turbine disaster, the vet came to treat Angus's wounds. Apart from some minor cuts, he was relatively unscathed from his misadventure. But, for years afterwards, whenever it was stormy or there was thunder and lightning on the go, he would take to standing knee deep in the middle of the duck pond staring intently into the corner of his field at something no one else but he could see.

8

A TRIP TO BUCKIE – 23rd August

Dod was well known to be fond of a drink. But in adulthood at least, he drew the line at fortified wine. He'd had the dubious pleasure of tasting a concoction called White Tornado during a football trip to Glasgow's East End as a teenager and had never quite forgotten the experience. It was during a pre-match drinking session in a spit and sawdust boozer near Celtic Park and the syrupy nectar was available on tap and by the pint or, providing you brought your own bottle, as a wee carry oot to take along to the game in your inside jacket pocket.

Legend has it that the noxious liquid was actually a mixture of cheap white wine from Portugal mixed in with the slops from customers glasses then fermented in a barrel to be sold back to them as fortified wine. Another legend insists that the concoction was originally used by the bar staff to clean the bar tops until the pub's owner realised that he could make more money from it by selling it over the counter.

And Scots comedian Billy Connolly famously described the fiery stuff as "pure gallus" and "what the Pope drinks when he runs out of Crème de Menthe". But it certainly wasn't to everybody's taste.

Aberdeen thrashed Celtic by three goals to two that fateful Saturday but Dod never made it to the match. He and a couple of school pals, Johnny Meerison and Tarn Gibb ended up on a park bench outside the stadium having been refused entry by the lads at the turnstile because they were too much the worse for drink.

> "Ye canny get in in that state boys!" they thundered. "Away and sober up and come back when you can string two words together!"

But it never happened. In fact, they only just made it to the supporters coach for the trip home that evening and the three of them slept most of the way North oblivious of the victory celebrations aboard the bus.

Both Johnny and Tarn recovered well from the experience and fortified wine became a staple of their weekends. But Dod never touched the stuff again. His life had taken a different path and university beckoned him. In sharp contrast, his two school pals were apprenticed to the local slaughterhouse. Johnny became a killer and Tarn worked a chainsaw on the cattle disassembly line. It wasn't a particularly pleasant occupation and there was a strong drinking culture to deaden the senses from the sounds and the smells of the doomed beasts. So, for Dod's two schoolmates, weekends on the batter quickly became the norm as a means of driving out the demons.

Buckfast was their wine of choice since you couldn't easily get White Tornado North of Coatbridge and Lanliq Fortified Wine, probably the next best alternative and known as Electric Soup, was seen locally as a bit down-market by the aficionados of Invermorrisay. At fifteen per-cent proof and a mere few pounds for a pint bottle it was a cheap enough way of getting steaming on a weekend bender. And the pair didn't seem to mind the sugary taste of the concoction which some wine critics have likened to a mixture of Cola and cough mixture with a whiff of gunmetal as a subtle aftertaste.

One reviewer even went as far as to suggest that the Vatican ought to send an exorcist over to Buckfast Abbey to scourge the place of that ungodly concoction made by Godly men! But neither Tarn nor Johnny cared tuppence about such scorn. All they were after was an escape from the daily grind and the wine gave them that and more at a price they could afford.

Every few years there would be a school reunion which Dod always attended. It was usually an evening affair in the toon hall with an accordion band and a bite to eat and a spot of dancing for those that wanted it. It was an opportunity to meet up with past classmates and find out what they had made of their lives since school and he always looked forward to it.

It was on one of these occasions that he chanced upon Johnny and Tarn. He'd not seen them for maybe twenty years and although they looked a bit the worse for wear, he could still see in their faces a faint glimmer of the days of long ago when nothing seemed impossible and the whole world seemed ripe for the taking.

Tarn still had his long black locks tied back in a pony tail under an ancient flat cap and as for Johnny, he still sported a goatee beard and the handlebar moustache he'd tended to as a teenager. Neither lad had married though Tarn had fathered a son and a daughter both of whom were now up and about and raising their own offspring somewhere up by Inverness.

> "I only see them at weddings and funerals and the like," he told Dod. "They have their own lives and their mum doesn't want anything to do with me nowadays. She was happy enough to collect the maintenance though. Always the way. But I'm better off on my own with no one to tell me what to do and what not to do."
>
> "How about you Dod?" asked Johnny. "Did you never consider settling doon?"

Dod looked thoughtful and was silent for a bit before replying.

> "Nah nah. Not for me. I did have a few relationships though. But they never came to much in the end and, you know how time flies past when

you're not looking. I suppose I'm much too set in my ways nowadays and who would have me anyway."

He laughed and downed a forkful of stovies before continuing.

"I still see Julie Lucas though. Not in that way of course. She's married with sons and comes into the library every few weeks. Sometimes wonder how that might have worked out. But its water under the bridge now."

At the next reunion, Johnny was missing. It had been all of ten years since the last meet-up and Tarn turned up alone. His pony tail was greying nowadays and the old flat cap was missing and he was balding from the forehead. But you could still tell it was him. As Dod approached, he looked up with a cheery smile.

"Fit like Dod? How's things? Long time no see!"
Dod sat down beside his old school pal.
" Time flies Tarn. Time fairly marches on. You just on your own? Half expected Johnny to be with you."

Tarn looked down at the table for a bit.

"He's gone Dod. It's been near three years now since he went. I assumed you might have heard."

Crestfallen and embarrassed that he hadn't known, Dod struggled for words.

"I'm really sorry to hear Tarn. No, I didn't know. How did he die if you don't mind me asking?"

Tarn looked puzzled for a second.

"Oh, he's not dead Dod. He's become a monk!"

It was Dod's turn to look puzzled.

"But I thought you said he had gone Tarn! How in blazes did he end up as a bloody monk?"
"Well," replied Tarn. "It was just after Christmas a year or so ago and we'd maybe had a tiny bit too much to drink all during the holidays

when I said to him that it would be fine to go and visit where they make the Buckfast. And, you know how one thing leads to another! So, we ended up planning a trip South. It was a sort of pilgrimage you understand. It was never meant to a religious sort of thing. I mean, neither of us had been near a priest or a church for as long as I can remember. Well, you know that already. We were just never into that sort of stuff even at the school."

Over the next hour Dod listened as Tarn blurted out bits and pieces of the story in between slurps of whisky and a few mouthfuls of stovies. It turned out that the pair had been on a bender lasting almost five weeks. They'd been suspended from work and advised to dry out or be dismissed for misconduct. It wasn't the first time this had happened and normally the threat of dismissal evaporated once they were sober and back on their game. But this time things were looking bleak and Johnny had spun his boss a story about how the pair were giving up the drink for good and how they were off to a religious retreat centre for a few weeks to get sorted out once and for all. They just needed more time and a bit of understanding.

The manager bought it. He was a Christian sort of chap and the story about the retreat centre held some appeal. Plus, they'd worked under him for as long as he could remember and he was loath to let them go. So, he gave them yet another benefit of the doubt and even agreed to give them leave on half pay for a few weeks to help them along on their journey to sobriety. But as is often the case when drink has a firm grip, things did not go exactly as planned.

First on the agenda was to get hold of a car and a driver. Tarn had never learned to drive and Johnny had lost his licence years before and never bothered applying to get it back. As it happened, a colleague on the killing floor had just retired and had spare time on his hands. For the price of the petrol and his bed and board along the way, he agreed to drive them to Buckfast Abbey the following week. They'd have to make their own way back though. He was heading off to London afterwards to visit relatives in Streatham and it might be weeks before he headed North again.

And that was Johnny Meerison's introduction to monastic life. The pair duly arrived at Buckfast, did the tour of the winery and stayed over at a local hotel for a couple of nights. Each morning after breakfast, they would head back to the monastery where, uncharacteristically, Johnny would spend his day sitting alone and silent in the chapel and Tarn would do the winery tour for the third or the fourth time before heading out into the grounds to polish off a bottle of the holy water under a tree. Finally, with the funds getting low, they headed home by train. But things in future were going to be very different between the two pals.

While Tarn occupied his time getting unca fu each day of the trip, Johnny had touched nary a drop. True, he'd sipped at his complimentary glass of Buckie at the end of the tour on day one. But after that he'd not shown any interest whatsoever in the hooligan wine. It was as if he'd had a Damascus Road experience. As if the well-watered cattle killer from Invermorrisay had changed his name to Paul. Which was, later on, exactly what he did.

> "When we got back home" recalled Tarn, "he was a completely changed man and began talking about taking holy orders. Soon he was spending weekends up in Elgin at the abbey at Pluscarden and before a year had passed, he'd become a novice and started off on the path to what he said was his true vocation. It was all a bit difficult to take in to be quite honest."

And so it was that Johnny Meerison, the killer at the slaughterhouse, became Brother Paul. A six-month postulancy led to a two-year noviciate. Monastic life with all its Psalms and its Latin and its Gregorian Chant replaced the blood-soaked aisles of the killing house and the perfumed stink of death that permeates that world.

The 6th Century Rule of St. Benedict became his mantra and finally, after a full five years had passed, Paul's Solemn Vows replaced his Temporary Vows and Brother Paul fae Invermorrisay solemnly and permanently committed himself to the monastic life and all that went along with it.

Neither Dod nor Tarn Gibb ever visited their school pal at the abbey. It just didn't seem right to intrude. Tarn spent the remainder of his working days at the abattoir before retiring to a caravan at Lossie to drink himself to death beside the seaside.

Dod wrote to Brother Paul a few times over the years and there was always a very kind but very brief reply. And, in a way, Dod was glad of that. It made things easier. After all, the man he knew fae school as Johnny Meerison no longer existed so it was probably best not to poke memories at a sleeping bear.

9

THE LAST GARDNER – 27th August

In what turned out to be a uniquely unlikely event, the early morning bus from New Mordrach to Peking via Kabul and Lhasa had suffered an engine fire just outside Invermorrisay. It was mid-afternoon when Dod chanced upon what remained of the drama. He'd been on his way back from the monthly purchasing meeting at Library HQ but instead of taking the regular return route had driven round by Quarthies to sup tea from his Thermos flask in a lay-bye before heading back to work for the remainder of the afternoon. But, just a few hundred yards from the familiar rest stop, a less familiar sight in the form of a smoke blackened double decker bus hove into view.

The local fire engine with its volunteer crew had come and gone and a local farmer, busy with his beasts today, had stopped past to offer help in the morn. The damage appeared more than just superficial.

A tractor would come next day to drag the bedraggled double decker back home to New Mordrach for inspection but in the meantime, the big red liveried London bus was parked up at the end of a farm track with a balding man in a pink summer dress tinkering loudly under the blackened bonnet with what sounded like a lump hammer.

As he thumped away at the engine block, he could be heard cursing loudly as whisps of black oily smoke emerged from underneath the cab. A pool of sump oil floated on top of the fire-brigade water around the front of the vehicle and the cursing mechanic's red patent leather sandals were now stained almost as black as the shiny leather handbag which lay open and discarded on the grass verge. A hairbrush, a mirror, a lipstick and a pair of soot blackened gloves had spilled onto the grass. And an oily, pink knitted cardigan hung abandoned on the hedge behind.

Curious, Dod pulled up alongside and got out to inspect the strange scene. There was a large cream coloured wooden destination board on the vehicle's upper deck. It read '153624 PEKING VIA KABUL & LHASA' in big black capital letters. Along one side of the advertising panel on the upper deck were the words 'NEVER UNDERESTIMATE A HEDGEHOG' and on the other side, 'DON'T BE FOOLED AGAIN OR AGAIN'. Clearly, thought Dod, this was not a regular country bus service.

"Do you need any help?" asked Dod as he approached the furious mechanic.

The red-faced man turned sharply. He paused before replying and, wiping his oil-stained hands on the hem of his dress, snarled tearfully.

"Does it look like it? Bloody thing went on fire!"

He then turned away and began hammering away at the engine again. By now the tarmac around the bus was littered with broken engine parts and a red stream of what looked like brake fluid began to turn the pool of engine oil underneath the bus a lurid pinkish brown to match the man's tights.

"Do you think that might help?" asked Dod softly, amused by what he saw but also mildly concerned at the man's behaviour.

"No" came the reply, "but it's taken me eight years to get here from the depot and now the ungrateful beast of a thing has let me down. We were supposed to be in China by the end of the year and now it's not happening! Twelve miles! Only twelve bloody miles! That's as far as we got. Just another 4,832 to go.

And that's the last Gardner bus engine as well! The factory closed in January and I moved heaven and hell to get my hands on the very last six-cylinder LXB to exit the production line just before the doors closed forever! No chance in hell of getting another! Bloody unreliable things anyway. Slightest fuel leak and up they go in flames! I suppose it's back to the depot for a major rethink."

Dod was intrigued and offered the man in the pink dress a lift home to wherever that was. Having made the offer, he hoped it wasn't too far. The angry mechanic thought for near half a minute before slamming down the bonnet of the bus with a final muttered curse. He turned to Dod and with an "aye that wid be fine", picked up his hat and his handbag and got into the passenger seat having thoughtfully grabbed a dry towel from the back of the bus to sit on.

"Where to?" said Dod.

Home turned out to be a caravan on a tummle-doon wee croft just a few miles over the hill just outside a tiny village. Now, New Mordrach for all its sma size, was a hotbed of curtain twitchers. You'd rarely meet a soul on either of the main streets, but barely a thing happened in the place without half the population kenning all about it. The ither half wid find out soon enough though since gossip wis king in the tiny wee toon. The lang winding main road revealed little of this though and the casual traveller might easily speed through the village without much in the way of a second thought.

Despite the observations of the windae spies, one carload of strangers at least had made it through the place without being spotted. It was after the botched robbery at the post office. The robbers had gotten away with just £32 from the purse of the post-mistress leaving her tightly bound and gagged in the wee flat high above the shop. The poor woman lay gasping unnoticed for hours then died of what the police said was asphyxiation. And all the time the entire weeks takings sat in plain view on the couch in a brown paper carrier bag unnoticed by the robbers.

There was a big murder hunt but it came to nothing. Despite the best efforts of the detectives, the case was never solved although the gossip mongers had already solved it several times over and for years the whispering fingers wagged away behind closed doors pointing blame at difficult neighbours.

The place was sort of midway between the bustle of Aberdeen and the sweaty fisher toons on the Moray coastline with soft rolling farmland on the Western side of toon and a muckle patch of peat moss over to the East.

A little narrow-gauge railway train ran fae the outskirts of the tiny place across to the peat workings a mile or so distant. It ran from dawn till near dusk most weekdays and half a day on a Saturday and spent its time hauling the soggy fuel to the drying stacks then clanking its way back along the wobbly track to bring more. Folks fae roon aboot never bothered much about the clanking and, if they thought much about it at all, would have maybe compared it to a birdsong or a roar of wee Grey Fergies. It was just a part of the naitral warld in these parts. Maybe some of them even missed the puffing billie when it stopped over in its tiny engine shed on the sabbath. But no one ever really said as much, at least not in public and certainly not to strangers. And Alastair, for that was the bus mechanic's name, was almost certainly an outsider in these parts.

When Dod and the still angry Alastair arrived at the croft, it was mid-afternoon. Dod had realised that he would have to make excuses for his absence and make up his time the next day. But, what the hell. How often do you stumble across a burnt-oot London bus in the wilds of the Aberdeenshire countryside accompanied by a mannie all dressed up like he wis aff tae the dancin on a Friday night? There had to be a back story here. And, as things turned out, there certainly was.

The tiny caravan had obviously seen better days and the croft house itself was just as bad. The building had lost its roof long ago. The front door and all the windows were lang-gane and the park at the back of the place was piled high with timber beams and breezeblocks just waiting maybe for a joiner or a stone mason to chance bye and take pity on the place. Dod noticed a big pile of green painted wooden doors at the back of the building but thought nothing more of it at the time.

"You'll be needing a drink of something will you? Come on in, were open all hours after all," said the mechanic in the summer dress.

And Dod nodded in response, expecting maybe a coffee or some rank herbal tea out of a cracked cup. But no, when he climbed the step into the wee caravan it was all spick and span and Alastair produced a box of red wine and two shiny clean glasses that looked as if they'd just come off the shelf at Asda. There was an elderly ginger cat on the only bed in the van and it was quickly shooed off to make way for Dod to sit down while Alastair pulled out a tiny folding chair at the other side of the table. Dod took a sip of the wine.

Then, curious, he asked "So, you're off to China then?"
"How the blazes did you know that?" snarled Alastair.
Dod took a deep breath before replying politely. "It's written on the front of your bus actually. Besides, you told me earlier when we were at the roadside."
Alastair reddened and looked down at the cat who by now had curled up at his feet. "I'm sorry. I'm just upset is all. It's been such a let-down. I'd hoped to be well away from this God forsaken place forever and now … well."

He lifted up the cat and took a slurp from his wineglass before continuing.

"It's a small Nazarene temple on wheels you see and now, after the fire, it'll take years to rebuild. In Chaldean numerology it equals nine. In Pythagorean numerology it's the sum of seven. The numbers 153624 represent the firing order. When I played Hamlet, everything was clear and now it's not. Don't you get it?"

The rambling monologue continued for almost ten minutes during which Dod struggled to remain calm in the face of this incoherent onslaught of words. There were references to obscure Christian sects mixed in with jumbled up Shakespearian quotes from a number of the bard's plays. Strings of numbers claimed to prove unintelligible theories about why the Lodekka bus had to get to a certain point in China in plenty of time prior to the third day of the Second Coming. And at one point the man in the pink dress began speaking in tongues to the cat. The ginger beast didn't seem particularly bothered and set about the more serious business of licking its wee pink erse as the rant continued. But Dod began to feel a rising sense of unease. It was maybe time to go before there were more surprises.

> "Milk in a refrigerator takes on the odour and the taste of the food next to it," continued Alastair, perhaps unaware that he had changed the subject completely. Then he raised his voice.
> "Everyone knows that! As scared or as ignorant as you might be, that is an unescapable truth! It's where our monsters came from after all. We all have a little sensor in our head to detect them. Either that or the monsters are in the wrong place. Don't you get the irony in all of that?"

Dod took an uncomfortable sip of his wine and realised that Alastair was almost certainly the maddest person he had met of recent and that his own curiosity had exceeded his sense of unease in the man's presence. He looked around for an easy escape should things take an unexpected turn and sensing that there really wasn't one decided to leave while he could via the half open caravan door. After promising to call back again in a few days, he made some flaccid excuses and squeezed quickly past the still seated Alastair who continued to rant to the cat.

A few weeks later he chanced by the croft on his way back from a trip to the coast. It was one of those end of summer August sultry days when the breeze was away bothering somebody else at the far end of the county and an end of day thunderstorm was likely on the way according to the weather forecast. He'd spent some leisurely hours watching the North Sea trawlers bobbing in the harbour and drinking coffee and reading some bits of Proust before heading home to eat and sleep and dream before the inevitable Monday morning shift at the issuing desk.

There was a sun-glassed man sitting in a deckchair amongst the long grass outside the front door of the croft. He was reading from a newspaper and looked up when Dod drove slowly up the lane. It wasn't Alastair as far as he could tell. Too tall perhaps and certainly far too blond and not wearing a dress and no obvious sign of make-up or high heels.

The caravan had gone and there, where it had once been, stood the big red bus still blackened from the engine fire and still sporting the wooden destination board with '153624 PEKING VIA KABUL & LHASA' painted on in big black capitals. And in the park at the back of the place the big pile of green doors had been dismantled and spread about on the grass in neat rows maybe six feet apart. And in between the rows, someone had erected lines of garden canes; hundreds of them. A faint evening breeze was stirring and he could see that the lines of canes were all linked by hundreds of yards of what could only be white toilet paper fluttering weakly in the dimming sun. The man in the deckchair waved and smiled as Dod pulled up.

"Are you a friend of Alastair?" said the tall blonde. "I'm afraid he's not here. Might not be back for a while!"

Dod wound down the car window. "I met him a few weeks back after the bus fire. Gave him a lift back here actually. I was just passing and wondered how things had gone. With the bus repair I mean. He seemed upset. I mean, very upset."

"Aye" agreed the blond man. "He was indeed. When they took him away, he made that very clear."

"Took him away?" replied Dod. "Can I ask where to?"

The blond man glanced down and smiled weakly and looked thoughtful for a minute. "I've maybe said too much already" he replied. "Tell you what though, if you give me your address, I'll pass it on to Alastair and he can maybe get in touch when he's a bit better. How does that sound?"

In for a penny thought Dod. He wrote his name and work address down on a page ripped from his work diary and handed it to the seated man. And with a polite thanks and a hand-wave, he wished the tall blond good evening then headed back down the lane wondering what, if anything, he'd gotten himself involved in.

It was some three weeks later when the first letter arrived from the hospital at Cranhill. Dod had not forgotten about the episode. In fact, he had made discreet but unfruitful enquiries about the man in the pink dress with the big red bus. The episode had never made the paper and the volunteers at the Fire Service could only confirm that they had indeed attended a vehicle fire on that road on that day and that they had extinguished it at the roadside. On top of that, all he had was a Christian name so a more extensive official search was nigh impossible. He had thought of asking locals at the village about the man with the bus. But had never followed through since it seemed intrusive. But the letter changed everything.

It was post-marked Peterhead and bore the return address of a psychiatric ward, Ward 14, at Cranhill Hospital and was signed 'Yours sincerely Alastair McGlone, Principal Conductor and Duty Learning Assistant Mechanic at Buchan International Transport Corporation Ltd Inc.'

"Dear George," it began.

"It is extremely uplifting that you see value in my small enterprise here in rural Buchan. Especially so at a time when various mechanical setbacks have again come to the fore. I hope that this letter finds you well and that it will go some way to explain the questions that you will undoubtably have regarding our chance meeting on the highway to the Orient all those weeks ago. It was a day when mechanical setbacks came to the fore and I myself have come to doubt that I will ever have anything significant to offer in our search for meaning in this life; though I shall press on regardless.

I had to close the depot prior to my incarceration here since visitor numbers had dwindled and all interest had drained away. In fact, the plan to drive the bus to the Orient has come to nothing and my attempt to attract a new audience has come to nothing also. The bus remains parked outside the croft and remains inoperative due to engine damage sustained as a result of both the fire and the failure of my temporary roadside repairs with what, in retrospect, may have been wholly inadequate tools.

I have not thrown in the towel yet however and am merely stepping back to focus on the next phase of my mechanical endeavour. I have made enquiries regarding a replacement engine and await a response from the Chief Engineer. This may take some time since these engines are not made anymore. But I am hopeful that there may yet be one last Gardner engine crated and awaiting collection at the factory for delivery to the depot for installation into the exhibit.

I would like very much to keep you informed of the progress and look forward to meeting up with you upon my discharge from this sad place should that ever happen. The timing of my return to the croft is uncertain at present. Perhaps you will agree to correspond by letter in the meantime.

Yours sincerely,

Alastair McGlone, Principal Conductor and Duty Learning Assistant Apprentice Mechanic at Buchan International Transport Corporation Ltd Inc."

On the face of it, the letter posed more questions than it answered. But at least it gave some clue as to the mental state of the writer and to his current whereabouts. Dod thought for a day or so before replying briefly but positively.

"Dear Alastair,

It was really heartening to hear from you. I did call past your home recently just to see how you were faring, but as we both know, you were not in residence at the time. It was kind of your friend to pass on my contact details.

It is heartening to learn that you plan to repair the bus. It must have been a shattering blow when the project came to a fiery halt at such an early stage in the journey. Perhaps, when you are able, we can meet up in the double decker to chat about your plans to resume your quest. I would like that very much.

Meantime, please keep in touch.

Kind regards,

Dod King (Senior Librarian, Invermorrisay Public Lending Library)"

It was some weeks later when the next letter arrived. The summer had gone out with a cold wet blast and the harvest had been blighted by the damp weather so much so that many of the smaller farmers had resorted to burning off the ruined barley in the parks rather than bear the cost of drying the grain for whisky.

Life at the library droned on as usual and, despite a long summer break from the lending and retrieving of other people's books, Dod found himself counting the days till his long-awaited retirement. He'd been writing and doing some gentle hillwalking on the days when he felt able. The Parkinsons was at an early stage but all the while he was dreading the return to work. Just four more years and sixteen days and four hours, he calculated. And with time off for sickness and holidays, three years and five months or even less. What's not to like he mused. He had almost, but not quite, given up on the story of the bus from New Mordrach to China when the second letter from the man in the pink dress arrived.

"Dear George," began the second letter.

"I am so sorry to be so slow in getting back to you as promised. It has been a very busy few months here and, health-wise, things are generally progressing quite well. I have come to strongly realise that there is a story to be told on the mechanical front and wonder if we might meet up on the lawn at the croft on my return.

You should understand though that I feel myself to be simply a supporting actor to the main players here and am not in any way at the centre of the action. It's simply that I was around at the time of these events and I do often wonder whether the key players are in fact my spirit guides to the ways of the world or, more correctly perhaps, my instructors in the ways of the universe. Time, if indeed there is such a phenomenon, will no doubt reveal all.

I have today tried to contact the former head of engineering at the Engine Works to see if he has any knowledge of a spare power plant to replace the ruined one. His name is Amos and I am hoping that he will have some good news on this front since without a replacement, there can be no onward journey towards the Orient. I hope you will understand my concerns.

Yours sincerely,

Alastair McGlone, Conductor and Associate Junior Transport Officiator First Class (Acting Only)"

Dod re-read this second letter then set it aside. Truth be told, he was unsure of what to make of it. The man was clearly still disturbed. It was several days later that he decided to reply. Again, as in his initial reply, he was short and to the point. Making no promises, he acknowledged Alastair's letter, wished him well and agreed to meet on the lawn at the croft at a time convenient to them both. Just a few days later, another Dear George letter arrived at the library.

"Dear George," it began.

"I quite sincerely hope this finds you well. I am now back at Grebe Croft and convalescing from what has proved to be a less than positive experience within the health system. There have been further setbacks on the mechanical front since we last spoke however and there are further structural defects on the bus which will require rectifying prior to setting off again to the East. Nonetheless, nothing in this material world is insurmountable and a solution is likely to be found to all of those issues. Remarkable people abound as I'm sure you agree and we must relentlessly challenge pre-conceptions wherever we encounter them.

If you are free next weekend, it would be fine to meet up on the bus for a chat. I shall be there from 10am on Sunday next and shall expect you to be prompt.

Yours sincerely,

Alastair McGlone, Former Conductor and Assistant Associate to the Chief Engineer (Now Retired)."

And that was it. No negotiation, just a summons. But in the light of what had gone on beforehand, a curious Dod turned up at the croft at the appointed time hoping to find some resolution to the story. It was a sunny morning and as he drove up the lane the tall blond man was there to welcome him.

"Hi, you must be George," said the blond. "Welcome! We've met briefly before, but maybe in better days. I'm afraid Alastair can't be here to meet with you. I'm Terry by the way. A friend of Alastair. I helped him from time to time with the croft and the with the overland project. That was before it all went belly-up of course."

Dod stared at the man, unsure what to say.

Terry continued "I don't know if you've heard, but Alastair passed the other day. It was by his own hand and to be honest it wasn't completely unexpected."

"I'm very sorry to hear that," said Dod. "Sorry for your loss."

Terry smiled. "Thank you. These things are never easy and even when you think you're prepared for them they take you completely by surprise. He'd been on the verge for years, hence the hospital admissions. But I suppose it's the finality of it all. He mentioned you specifically in his suicide letter and asked me to have a chat. I hope you don't mind."

"Goodness!" exclaimed Dod. "What kind of chat? I barely knew the man."

Terry looked thoughtful. "All I know is that he left instructions asking me to relate his story. Fill in the blanks sort of stuff. I guess he must have taken a shine to you or something. Shall we have a seat in the bus, I think its maybe about to rain."

It wasn't about to rain. In fact, the skies were completely cloudless which was a rarity in these parts. But Dod nodded dutifully. And with that, the pair set off down the park to where the broken bus sat on the lawn and took their places on the long green buttoned leather bench seats on the lower deck.

It was the first time Dod had been inside the converted bus. Up front, just behind the driver's cab there was a tiny galley kitchen next to a small solid fuel Rayburn stove. A set of smoke blackened aluminium pans hung from hooks above the tiny sink and a small gas-powered fridge hummed gently underneath the red Formica worktop. The remainder of the forward passenger area had been converted to house a fold-down dining table and there were two thin bunk beds built into the mid-section. Several slim aluminium stowage bins were dotted round the interior and the general appearance was one of pleasant but cluttered austerity.

The pair exchanged some awkward pleasantries about the view over to the peat-lands and such like. Then Terry began to speak at length.

"I'm not really sure where to start to be completely honest." he began. "But here goes. And feel free to stop me if you've heard it already since I'm not entirely sure how much Alastair has already told you."

The tale took up the next two hours as Dod sat spellbound. After a little while, he pulled out a notepad and began openly taking notes. Terry seemed unphased by this and it occurred to Dod that the man was unburdening himself of a guilty secret. Seeking forgiveness even. It was all very intense and he couldn't help but wonder what this confessional was leading to. Was Alastair really dead? Or was Terry maybe just another drug addled hippy on some vague road to nowhere?

At just after midday, Terry's monologue came to an abrupt stop. Announcing that he'd said all that he could say at present, he stood up and pressed the bell before theatrically announcing that this was Dod's destination for the day.

> "I'll be in touch," he shouted as the stunned Dod made his way back to his car. "I'm really sorry. I'll give you a call in a week or so and give you the rest of the story."

And with that, Terry closed the door of the bus and disappeared from view. In a way, it was exactly what Dod had expected so he gritted his teeth and reluctantly drove off to await the next summons.

It was some weeks before Dod got around to reading his notes from the encounter. Library life had been busy and he'd barely had time to eat and sleep between all the early and all the late shifts. It was also flu season and there were staff shortages all around the county. On top of that, a new computerised library system was being trialled at the Invermorrisay branch to replace the tried and tested card index system. Chaos and confusion ruled alongside a natural staff resistance to the implementation of the new ways. The notion that a machine could outperform experienced professionals seemed ridiculous to some and even Dod had begun to have his doubts.

There were days when the new system failed to operate at all and staff were forced to call in the technical guys from headquarters to sort out the mess. On other days it worked like a dream leaving some in fear for their jobs. But all things pass and by autumn Dod's work life balance returned to normal and he found himself with more time for the writing.

The day after his birthday, a Saturday in September, he sat down to write up his notes from his morning meeting with Terry at Glebe Croft.

According to Terry, Alastair had been born near Manchester in 1936 or

1937. His mother was an army nurse who hung herself when he was ten. He'd never known his father and, throughout his time in care, he would tell anyone who asked that his dad had been a war hero and a high-ranking officer in the RAF. It wasn't true. But the fantasy provided some much-needed comfort to the broken child.

After National Service, Alastair took some time out to travel part way along what would in later years become known as the hippie trail. India beckoned and there were early beginnings of an overland route by Magic Bus through Tehran, Herat, Kandahar, Kabul, Peshawar and Lahore then on to Uttar Pradesh. The bus he and his companions were travelling on only got as far as Istanbul where, following a mechanical breakdown, the travel company abandoned them and the group took up temporary residence in the slums of the Sultanahmet.

Gradually his fellow passengers drifted off. Some to Australia. Some to Greece. And some to a drug induced state of enlightenment in some commune or other along the trail. Probably a very few of them eventually reached their intended destination. But Alastair was certainly not one of them. After spending a couple of weeks living in a stinking flea infested room above the Pudding Shop on Divan Yolu, he headed back the way he had come spending the dregs of his savings on a one-way ticket on a West bound Magic Bus to, of all places, Aberdeen.

A series of mundane jobs later, he found himself in possession of a block of London flats in Mayfair. A blood relative whom he had never met since childhood had died and Alastair was sole beneficiary. Alongside the rental income there was a sum of money. Enough to buy a dress shop!

It was the seventies and when young folk got their Friday pay packet, they often made a beeline for Union Street to buy a wee skirt or a sparkly top in preparation for a night at the dancing. Alastair's big idea was to pile 'em high and sell 'em cheap. There were regular 'Everything Must Go' and 'Closing Down' sales and for a time the punters and the profits rolled in. It all went well for a year or so until the Revenue and the relentless cost cutting caught up with Al's Bargain Fashion Emporium. While the clothes were cheap and cheerful, the downside was that they rarely lasted more than a few washes before completely falling apart. And, due to an accounting oversight, Alastair had omitted to attend to the legal requirement to pay tax on his sales.

It wasn't unusual to have a line of unhappy customers outside the shop door on a Monday morning queuing for refunds and holding up soleless shoes or busted handbags. The business was in terminal decline and the emporium was closed for good after a successful and quite genuine 'Closing Down – Everything Must Go' January sale in 1972.

Bruised by the experience, Alastair had licked his wounds, paid his dues to the revenue and retreated to his croft in the countryside along with the remaining stock. The rental income from the flats in Mayfair was still pouring in and all he needed was time to plan a new business venture to invest in. It was then that he'd met up with Terry.

In late October, Dod was summoned to the croft for what he hoped might be the final time. This time it was raining and the bus windows were dripping condensation onto the leather seats as the pair settled down to continue with Alastair's tale. Pleasantries were duly swapped and Terry revealed more about the planned overland adventure.

"I'd been working offshore as a mechanical engineer" recalled Terry "and Alastair was my next-door neighbour across the field. We'd chat occasionally down the pub. Mainly about his plans to do up the croft house and maybe start a new business. He was an interesting character. Always well turned out and always ready to stand his hand."

"When you say well turned out, do you mean …" asked Dod.

"No. Not that," replied Terry. "Not at first anyway. That all came out much later. New Mordrach is maybe not the easiest place to engage in cross-dressing. I mean, folk might find it really difficult to accept. They just wouldn't really understand. That's not to say that Alastair maybe wore a pair of tights or a scanty pair of knickers under his jeans. I don't know really. It never really concerned me. But after we bought the bus, he seemed much more relaxed about his dress sense."

Dod looked up from his notes, "Oh yes, the bus! I'd like to know more about that."

"Nothing much to tell really," continued Terry. "He'd always intended doing another overland trip and the big idea was to kit out a restored double decker as a motor home and drive it overland to India. Simple as!

He had a route planned out although that kept changing over the years due to wars and politics and things. But essentially it was to be a wing and a prayer type of enterprise.

Eventually he set his sights on China but it could just as easily have been anywhere else in Asia. Privately though, I began to suspect that he never really intended to follow through with the actual journey but I never faced him with this since the planning and the work involved in modifying the bus seemed to keep his demons at bay."

There'd been an old London bus for sale at auction in Dundee. Some transport enthusiast or other had trundled off to bus heaven and his vehicle collection went under the hammer alongside a vast array of public transport ephemera. Uniforms, ticket machines, engine parts, that sort of thing. Terry and Alastair had filled an Asda bag with cash and taken the train to the auction. It was quite poorly attended and prices were rock-bottom. For just a few hundred pounds they not only got the bus, but returned home with enough spare parts to drive the thing to Mars and back which was just as well since the old vehicle had barely made it as far as the croft when, with a bang and a splutter and a burst of black smoke, the gearbox imploded.

"There's a popular myth," explained Terry "that public service vehicles are always a good buy because the bus companies keep them well maintained. But in reality, they tend to run them until it's not really worth maintaining them any longer. Then they sell them on to the highest bidder at auction. It's the same with police cars and fire engines. We kind of knew that to be honest and were surprised to make it all the way from Dundee before it broke down if truth be told.

We'd planned to go halfers on the restoration project but to be honest it was Alastair who picked up most of the bills. I lost my job when the oil went down and he pretty much paid for everything after that. He didn't really seem to mind as long as I mucked in with the build. It was then," said Terry "that he began to be more daring with the cross-dressing. You'd maybe find him in the caravan in his leopard-skin thigh boots and not much else, putting on his makeup. On one occasion, I arrived to find him in a bikini on the lawn sipping champagne and listening to jazz. There was nothing overtly sexual about it all. It was just Alastair being himself. After a while, I never really took much notice of his appearance. You just got used to it. But then the police got wind of it all."

It was at that point that Terry again abruptly ended the interview and ushered Dod out of the bus saying he'd be in touch very soon.

In late October a note from Terry arrived in the post.

"Dear Dod,
I hope that you are well and I apologise for the extreme delay in re-establishing communications with yourself. Should this little project of ours still be of even moderate interest to yourself, you are cordially invited to join us on the bus at our little depot on Glebe Croft this coming Saturday at 2pm prompt.
Kind regards,
Terry"

In for a penny yet again, thought Dod and he reluctantly swapped his Saturday library shift for two evening sessions midweek. When he arrived, there was no-one to be seen. The bus sat empty on the lawn still showing smoke damage from the fire and the caravan had reappeared and was parked alongside the house. He sat for a few minutes then tooted his horn. A few more minutes passed. Then the caravan began to move slightly and the door opened to reveal Terry still in his pyjamas.

"Give me a few minutes to get dressed" he shouted before disappearing back inside.

A half hour went by. Eventually Dod tried the bus door and made his way up the narrow winding stairs to the top deck. There, curled up on the front seat was the cat. He sat down on the seat beside it expecting it to at least look up or purr or do those things that cats are supposed to do. But the animal paid him little notice. Finally, it stirred and stared at him intently for perhaps a minute. Then, seeing no particular threat nor benefit in Dod, drifted off again to that land of chattering teeth and tasty bunnies and screaming birds that cats inhabit when they dream. There was the sound of footsteps on the metal stairs and Terry reappeared, fully dressed now and bearing a tray of coffee and toast. He put the tray down on the seat behind and sat down beside the cat.

"I see you've met Vicious Sid. He's not very friendly, is he? Alastair's cat really. Only hangs around to get fed. Normally won't let me anywhere near him. Growls if you get too close. Fluffy little sociopath really. Kills everything he sees. Even catches squirrels. Eats everything but the tail. Don't know what Alastair saw in him."

"Aye," replied Dod "I got your note."

Terry beckoned to the tray then got straight down to business. "Help yourself to milk and sugar. Now where did we get to?"

"The police." said Dod.

"Ah yes. The police," confirmed Terry.

The restoration had been going ever so slowly. Alastair was having trouble with the planning authority as well and he had stopped his tablets again.

"I can't drink AND take my medication!" he would say. "And I can't think clearly without my red wine!" "It was a familiar pattern." recalled Terry "and the planners only added to the downward spiral."

He continued.

"There was some sort of dispute over access you see. The council apparently owned the track alongside the croft and wanted a fee for access rights. Alastair could have easily written a cheque to settle the matter but refused to pay on principle. The result was an impasse. The croft-house remained uninhabitable and Alastair remained living in his caravan.
He'd been sectioned several times before and it became obvious that he was exhibiting delusional behaviour yet again." recalled Terry. "You probably saw the doors?"

Dod nodded.

"Well," continued Terry, "he'd bought a job lot of ninety-eight second hand wooden doors at a council auction and had them piled up the park alongside the croft. The delivery folk must have suspected he was barking mad and they would have been quite correct. One rainy night he began laying them out in neat rows across the field and the next day he went and bought a car load of garden canes and toilet rolls. You maybe saw them on your last visit."

Dod nodded again.

"Well, not to put too fine a point on it, he was in the midst of a manic episode and probably imagined that he was in front of an audience at the Albert Hall or somewhere similar. Once he'd erected the lines of canes, he festooned them with the toilet paper, put on some loud Straus and did a sort of dance of the seven loo rolls around the field. When the police arrived, the grass was covered with soggy toilet paper and Alastair had collapsed exhausted at the caravan door."

"Did they arrest him?" asked Dod.

"Well not at first." resumed Terry. "He was all boozed up and dressed up like Salome in the Straus opera. So that must have whetted their appetite, but it wasn't an offence. But they had been out looking for a missing child, a thirteen-year-old from the village, and lo and behold she turned up asleep but drunk on the top deck of the bus.

The two officers arrested Alastair on a charge of supplying alcohol to a minor and, to cut a long story short, he ended up being sectioned. There was never any suggestion that his intention was to harm the child. But she certainly could have come to harm accidentally. I mean, he was completely off his medication and quite manic by that stage. He accused the policemen of being nuns and told them that he was actually John the Baptist in disguise and that they should remove his head and maybe arrest his kneecaps to stop him escaping. So that gives you some measure of his mental state. "

Dod looked quite shocked. "So, what happened next?"

"Well," said Terry. "He gradually improved and they moved him to an open ward. He was back on all of his medication and at first all seemed well until one day, just a week following the move, he was found in a linen cupboard. He'd hung himself. End of story."

Weeks later, Dod found himself making a familiar detour through New Mordrach on his way North to visit his old pal James over in Buckie. There had been nothing more from Terry in the meantime and his curiosity had gotton the better of him. As he drove slowly up the lane leading to the old croft-house he saw that both the caravan and the bus had gone. The house was still derelict though and the field full of green doors had given way to a field laden with tall swaying grass sprinkled with bees and butterflies.

All that remained of the Silk Road overland adventure was a few scraps of pink cotton dress flapping limply from an old fence post and some faded black lettering on a broken wooden notice board nailed above the cottage door which read 'BE FOOLED AGAIN.'

He thought he smelled a faint whiff of cologne in the air though. Although it might have just as easily have come from the honeysuckle that ran along the entire length of the dubby lane.

He half expected to see Terry or even Alastair sunning themselves in the overgrown front garden. And try as he might, Dod could never quite shake off the notion that either Alastair was in fact Terry or that Terry was perhaps Alastair in some sort of clever disguise and that all the story telling was just some smoke and mirrors conjured up by a madman. As he headed off back down the lane, Dod felt a slight bump as he ran over the cat. But he was too deep in thought to pay it much attention.

A year or so later, when Dod was driving back from yet another trip to visit his pal in Buckie, he chanced upon a pair of hitchhikers raising a thumb to passing motorists. The tall one with the long blond wig wore a low cut bright yellow floral summer dress with black polka dots and a broad patent leather waistband. His shorter, but balding, companion sported a more modest calf length pink outfit with matching bodice and shiny pink ankle boots. Despite the obvious temptation, Dod didn't even bother to slow down.

10

MILKIE GEORDIE - 30th August

According to the Invermorrisay Reference Library copy of Encyclopaedia Britannica, Zanzibar is a semi-autonomous archipelago situated off the coast of Tanzania consisting of Zanzibar Island (locally named Unguja), Pemba Island and a great many smaller islands. Unguja is approximately 90km long and 30km wide which is roughly the size of the Isle of Skye.

The Britannica entry helpfully notes that in 1896 Zanzibar was the location of the world's shortest war, surrendering to British warships after 38 minutes of naval bombardment and that it is also one of the few places in the world where nutmeg is produced. The information was requested by library regular Geordie McGrath the milkie. But, for the love of God, the library staff were hard put to work out why the young lad was needing a run down about the tiny East African archipelago.

The man was a frequent borrower but his tastes were generally more to do with crime fiction of the worst kind and pulp fiction cowboy adventures. Dod decided to investigate the matter further. It wasn't really any of his or the libraries business, but his curiosity had gotten the better of him.

He recalled the last meaningful conversation between the two of them. It had involved that sudden death over at New Mordrach when old Dod Mutch was found slumped in his chair. It was Geordie who'd found him although on questioning about how he felt following the discovery of the body, the milkie seemed more upset about the three weeks milk money still owing than he was about the demise of the old one-armed bandit. No matter. It was worth pursuing.

Chance came on the following Tuesday. Geordie was in the habit of coming in past the library after he completed his round and, often as not, would arrive with a half full carton of milk in his hand which he would present with a flourish to the clerk at the issuing desk. The library clerk would dutifully thank him as if for the first time ever. And Geordie would typically reply that they were "very welcome indeed!"

> "We're allowed up to eight burst cartons a day you see. Maybe a bit more in winter because you're more likely to slip on the ice. I just thought you might like this one for the staff room."

The interaction rarely varied and there was always a reluctance to break the spell since the milkie seemed blissfully unaware that the exact same exchange had occurred the previous week, and the one before, and the one before that as well. In fact, in some ways the normality of the event became just another part of the weekly routine and if for some reason the milkie failed to appear with his leaking carton, it became a hot topic for discussion during break-times.

This particular Tuesday, Dod made sure that he was on the desk when the milk float drew up outside the library door. With the formalities regarding the burst milk carton over, Dod gently but firmly asked after Geordie's dad.

"How's your dad these days? I heard he'd had a wee stroke a few weeks hence" said Dod.

"Not so good to be honest, and thanks for asking. He's still in the ward" came the reply.

"So what's the story? Is he improving?" replied the librarian.

"He's been in for near four months now. My mum fairly misses him though. But she's not that great herself. Gets fair confused you see, and anxious as weel. She never really leaves the house. I tried taking her over the road to the pub once, just to get her out of the house you see, but she kind of panicked and just wanted back to her kitchen."

"Which ward is he in Geordie?" asked Dod.

"Which ward? I dinna really ken. I've not been in since he went away you see. It's my sister and ma auntie Madge what does all the visiting and they'd tell me if he wis getting ony worse."

"So you've not visited your dad since he went in?"

Geordie thought for a bit "Well, the ambulance came joost efter midnight. I mean, I had an early start. And, I had my mum to take care of as well you see! And, it's a lang trail into Aiberdeen an back as weel."

This time it was Dod's turn to pause and reflect. This was not the direction he had expected the exchange to go. But, in for a penny ...

"Ok. Have you considered going to see him? Maybe just to cheer him up. Maybe take him a few things. A book or a newspaper maybe? I'm sure he'd be really glad of the company."

He wondered if he'd gone too far with the interrogation but, the intrepid Geordie appeared not to notice the change of tone.

"Well, as ah said, my auntie visits and keeps in touch most weeks and ma sister as weel. You see, you eens dinna understand how hard this milk delivery job can be. You're up real early every day and after your work's done, you go for your pintie at five o clock. And then it's time to hae your tea. Then there's The Bill at seven."

Dod looked the young milkman straight in the eye. "The Bill?"

"Aye. There's the catch-up at the weekend of course, but it's nae quite the same. Better to watch it during the week when it's fresh. Then it's time for bed and back up the next mornin. Its nae easy to get tae the middle o Aiberdeen when there's all that gaun on. It's an early start you see, ah need to be in at the depot for 3.15am sharp to pick up my load otherwise I might get clocked! An I'm nae needing my wages docked. At wid be a bit o a disaster you see!"

A few weeks later the old man died in the City Hospital. There was a short piece in the local paper about him. Seems he had been injured while retreating through Dunkirk in 1940. Undertakers usually ask about pacemakers and anything with batteries which might explode during a cremation, but a German bullet lodged in the bum attracts little interest after all those years. There was another wee bit at the back of the paper in the obituary section. Paid for by the family, it simply read "Died peacefully following a short illness. Sadly missed".

As for Zanzibar. It remains one of the few places in the world where nutmeg is produced and still holds the record as being the location of the world's shortest war. But for the life of him, Dod never solved the mystery of why the milkie wanted to find out about the place. In fact, he never even asked if he'd made that final visit to that distant bedside in far off Aberdeen. It hardly seemed worth the effort of asking.

AUTUMN

Colourfu, Weet Wiks

11

PRACTICAL AIRSHIP HANDLING - 5th September

Another one of Dod's Wednesday Junior Library children's history readings involved gasbags. It was well attended. His reputation as a story teller had been greatly enhanced by that tale about how you could use a lobster's fart to make a rudimentary spirit level and his habit of bringing along a big box of biscuits ensured that his young audience would hang around at least until they could see their faces reflected on the bottom of the tin.

"Have you heard the tale about the big silver gasbags over at Lenabo?" he began.

Predictably, no one present had. So, he began to tell the tale.

"Now. In 1915 an army of labourers and mechanical diggers arrived at Longside in Buchan to build an airbase for naval airships at a place called Lenabo. It was wartime and despite the best efforts of the British Navy, the North Sea was infested with enemy submarines which were heading out into the Atlantic to prey on merchant ships. So, the big idea was to spot and, if possible, destroy the submarines from the air using airships.

They were called gasbags by the crews because they were full of a lighter than air gas called hydrogen which allowed them to float in mid-air. And they had a couple of big smoky diesel engines slung underneath to drive them forward using propellers. There would be a crew of maybe three including an engineer and a rack of bombs for the men on board to drop by hand if they spotted an enemy submarine."

Dod produced some photographs of the Longside airships which were duly passed around the munching children. Then he continued.

"It was never a success and, if truth be told, not a single German U-Boat was ever intercepted. One of the Longside airships, often known as silver sausages or Lenabo Soo's, was lost at sea. But despite wild theories about it being shot down in flames during some heroic action against a German submarine, the chances are that the ungainly thing simply ran out of fuel and crashed into the waves, killing all of the crew. Another crashed at Peterhead. But this time no one was killed and fisher-folk down at the harbour, seemingly watched with great amusement as a gang of naval ratings struggled to load the gas filled monster onto a truck for the journey back to Longside to be repaired and re-filled.

Now, as military bases tend to do, the airship base at Lenabo published a monthly magazine for the servicemen and women who were stationed there. It was titled 'The Battle Bag', and the Longside magazine was heavily censored and only ever contained poems and short stories along with adverts for the local toon hall tea dance or the latest Charlie Chaplin film at the Peterhead Palace Cinema.

Most editions are long gone. But one copy of the base magazine somehow made it into the dusty archives of the Library Service and, during an annual stock-taking, I stumbled upon it. It was printed by a printer called Scroggie and Sons in Peterhead and priced at sixpence in old money.

The library copy is dated September 1917 It has a cover image by an airman named as Richard Brock and features an anonymous article titled: 'Lectures on Serious Subjects No.3 - Practical Airship Handling'."

Dod paused to pass the sole surviving copy of The Battle Bag magazine around the room. Then he continued.

"As I said, the main article in this edition of The Battle Bag magazine is titled 'Practical Airship Handling' and I thought I'd read it out since its quite funny really."

Dod retrieved the Battle Bag and began to read out loud.

"1. A careful study of the various fatal aircraft accidents will show that these accidents have in the main been down to the unfortunate airman coming down too quickly.

2. Airship pilots should always remember that no matter how high they may be, they are bound to come down again, so why hurry. The trouble is getting up. Of course, by far the safer plan is not to go up at all. But the average young pilot, once he has made a fatal mistake, never stops to think. Hence Lecture Topic No.3.

3. Before making an ascent, the pilot should satisfy himself that the envelope is completely gas tight. Should a leak be suspected, careful search for same should be made with a lighted candle. If he comes to in hospital it was a leak. If he doesn't, it was still a leak.

4. It frequently happens that an airship proves to be so light that she will not descend. There are several immediate actions in an emergency of this kind. If possible, the airship should be got over

on her back so that the lift acts in a downward direction.

Should the crew be insufficient to do this, a man should be sent down the trail rope to look for extra ballast. Or, if the trail rope is not long enough, a sufficient number of men should be ordered up top to push her down.

In an emergency of the reverse order, where the ship loses lift and commences falling, one or more men should be sent up on top with orders to hold her back a bit. Or a ship can very often be stopped when falling if all the crew blow vigorously and simultaneously on the under part of the envelope.

As a last resort, if falling excessively rapidly, the lenses should be removed from the ships binoculars and the sun's rays focussed thereby on the envelope with a view to raising the temperature and consequently the lift of gas. Should the sun not happen to be out, an electric torch or luminous watch may be substituted.

5. In the event of an engine breaking down, efforts should be made to coax it to go again, either by hanging out a tin of petrol on a stick just in front of the propeller or by making a noise like a new magneto. If she doesn't go, then it's a pity.

6. Should the airship be making no headway, although the propeller appears to be revolving alright and there is no wind against you, stop and restart the engine and cut down your wine bill.

7. Instances have unfortunately occurred of pilots falling out of their airships. Should a pilot have the misfortune to do this, great care should be taken to select the spot on which he wishes to land. A sitting position is best. Early experiments with father will have taught him that this position presents the best natural shock absorber.

If on nearly reaching the earth he discovers that his attitude is inconvenient, or that a lightning conductor is immediately beneath him, then a fresh start should be made.

8. In every known instance of an airship going on fire while in mid-air, careful investigation has established that the cause was due to something having become ignited. In the event of such a catastrophe, the pilot should, after endeavouring to persuade himself that he is a hero, tidy his hair and look his best for a posthumous portrait in the London Times.

9. Should an airship burst apart in mid-air, the pilot should immediately turn out his pockets and destroy any letters or other documents he would prefer were not discussed at the inquest. Other details will be attended to by the authorities.
Should the rudder control wires come off the drum. It's no use getting pink in the face about it. Either give up boxing or other forms of physical training, or increase the strength of the airship parts.

10. An airship may sometimes become unmanageable due to complete rudder breakdown. If satisfied that a repair cannot be made, the pilot should forcibly bring the compass needle to the desired position and lash it fast to the ship. In its ultimate efforts to again take up a line parallel to the magnetic meridian, the needle will be found to swing the ship round with it, and full speed can then be made for home.

11. No effort should be spared, in the event of getting lost in a fog to locate your position as soon as possible. This can best be done by opening up both engines to full speed and forging straight ahead. You are bound to strike something familiar sooner or later.

12. But in all cases of emergency, presence of mind is of first importance. No man has ever died who retains his presence of mind! If only pilots would remember this!"

The reading seemed to go down well enough with the youngsters and after a few questions and some general discussion about modern alternatives to lighter than air hydrogen, the children headed off home to tell their parents about how Dod the librarian had taught them that the best way to identify a gas leak was to use a lighted candle to find the source.

Inevitably there were complaints and Dod received an official warning, not for the first time, about his outrageous behaviour.

> "Jesus, man! What on earth were you thinking! You can't go about telling young children how to blow themselves up with gas! You're on a final warning. If anything like this happens ever again, you'll face immediate suspension! Now close the door on your way out."

As Dod exited the library managers office, a mischievous little voice in his head whispered "Aye-aye Dod. Only 1,869 days to go before you can retire! Now that's not a lot, is it?"

12

THE SECRET SUNDAY CLUB – 10th September

The back-shop at Pattersons was another one of Dod's occasional hangouts. It was only open on a Sunday between the hours of 4pm and midnight and even then, only on those particular Sundays when auld Patterson's new blonde wis away visiting relatives in her native Glasgow which wis maybe once a month in summer and less often in the winter when like as not, the roads were slippery with ice and getting into Aberdeen for the train down South could prove to be a problem. According to Patterson, young Annie, who wis nearly thirty summers his junior, would never in a month of Sundays suspect that, on her weekends away, he held court in the back-shop to a bunch of drink-weary local lads.

But according to everyone else at Clacharty and all roon aboot as well, she didnae care a hoot about his nefarious habits and in any case wis off tae Barrowland wi a bunch of her pals for a wild weekend at the dancing. Wird wis she'd only married him to get the shop when he deet and she'd a fancy man just biding his time in the Gorbals waiting for the word to move in with her at the shop.

There was really no other reason she would have married sic an old mannie said the gossip. There were far too many years between them and he was past his best lang before she'd even met in with him. It must just be a waiting game to grab his money once he wis awa. There was no other reasonable explanation and that's a fact.

And, sure enough, the auld mannie was still warm in his grave when Jock Campbell fae Glasgow arrived in the village in his big blue Volvo Amazon saloon car and moved straight in to live with Annie in the flat above the grocer shop. Before long the pair were married and before much longer, she was pregnant with twins and by the following winter all the gossip had died down and things returned to what professed to be normal in the sleepy wee place where everybody talked about everybody ahint their backs and they all gloried in what they thought they knew even if there wis no truth in it at all. In truth, nobody really cared what Annie and Jock got up to as long as it made for a juicy bit of gossip. But there were occasional murmurs about the lack of a dram on a Sunday and eventually Jock caved in to local pressure and reinstated the Sunday shebeen in the back shop.

You had to be vouched for to get in of course. But that was never a problem and most times, providing you were willing to stand your hand, an invite from a neighbour or a nod from a regular was sufficient to gain entry to the secret Sunday pub. Even the local bobby was in on the act and once he'd crossed the threshold that first time, he really had little choice but to keep stum for fear of losing his job and maybe even his police pension. Rumour was that the authorities generally turned a blind eye anyway and, aside from the very occasional well publicised raid on such establishments, the powers that be tended to leave them alone. That was until Jock fae Glasgow rocked the boat.

When the twins came, everything had changed between Jock and Annie. Her days at the dancing were behind her and she took to motherhood like a deuk to water. Most weekdays were split between looking after the two girls and running the shop. And, when the twins were old enough to travel, she'd be off down to Glasgow to show them off to grannies and grandpas and aunties. Jock rarely accompanied her on these expeditions. Pleading truthfully that the shop needed manning, even on a Sunday, usually got him off the hook and over the years the pair drifted on with life but in different directions.

By the time the twins were in secondary school, things had settled into a pattern. Most weekends, Annie and the girls would head off down to Glasgow on the Friday night and most weekends, the threesome would return on the Sunday in time to bed down before the week ahead. But, one weekend, right bang in the middle of the summer holidays, they all went off on the Friday and never came back.

There was the usual parade of difficult phone calls and lawyer's letters and before he knew it, Jock fae Glasgow was single again. Aside from a frosty meeting on the day Annie came to collect her stuff, he never had much in the way of contact with the threesome ever again. The maintenance cheques flowed South as regular as clockwork over the years but the access arrangements were underused. Bitter from the split, Jock preferred to act as if the entire episode had never happened. He took out loans and bought the shop from Annie before settling into life as a rural shopkeeper come Sunday publican once again.

Now, it so happened that most of the original characters that had attended Sunday pub in auld Patterson's time had moved on down the hill to the churchyard and there was a new crowd on the go. There was Davy and Robbie and Sandy and a lad named Pete who owned the local garage. It was Pete who had put up most of the money for the shop but all was not well at Clacharty Motors. Petrol sales had collapsed when the big supermarkets had opened up in nearby Invermorrisay and a bit of dodgy dealing in vehicle testing certificates had cost Pete his MOT operator's licence. By all accounts, as a career criminal at least, he was a sandwich short of a picnic and on top of the MOT scandal, he'd been caught red-handed selling red diesel to a neighbour. He'd narrowly avoided court on that occasion and now he needed a fresh source of income. In short, Pete was not an ideal business partner. But beggars can't always be choosers and like it or not, Jock the shop was in debt to Pete the garage for more than he cared to think about and there was no getting away from that fact.

As for Davy and Robbie Soutar, well they were just ordinary working lads nearing retirement age who came in most weekends, supped whisky for a few pleasant hours then left to get up at dawn on the Monday to labour at the local livestock mart. They were by all accounts brothers but you'd never have known it from looks alone. One was tall and thin with a big blaze of Viking red hair. The other short and broad and bald as a badger's airse. There was maybe two years between them and rumour had it that when their mother went to register them at the council offices, she had difficulty with the question on the form that asked who the father was. A pedantic registration clerk had pressed her for an answer to the question.

"Surely you have some idea who the father is Mrs Soutar?" he asked.
"How in the blazes should I ken? Ye big dunderhead!" came the indignant response. "It could be ony one of a number o chiels! God Almighty, I canna keep track o all my mannies! Jist put Oon Kent on the bluidy form!" And that was exactly what he did.

Cattle and sheep were their only topics of conversation and most folk left them alone to get on with their cribbage or their cards or whatever board-game they chose to get engaged with on a Sunday at Jock's back-shop. Jock, for his part, was happy to take their money and the rest of the regulars were apt to be polite but distant towards the pair.

Sandy on the other hand was a much more interesting lad. Technically described as an Idiot Savant, a nicer lad you couldn't hope to meet. Even when worse for wear, he could be relied on to recite word for word the entire dialogue of every Hollywood film he'd ever seen. He knew the names of all the stars and could, if pressed, recall each and every name on the credits screen with cross-references to every other film he'd seen them in.

A favourite, but good natured, sport for the regulars was to think up some obscure question that he couldn't possibly answer. But Sandy was rarely lost for words. Providing he'd actually sat through a screening of the film in question, he was never wrong no matter how long ago he'd viewed it.

One Sunday in early March, Davy Soutar came in alone. When Jock asked about the whereabouts of his brother, he only said "He's been nae weel. I've left him his food on the bedside table. He's been nae weel the whole week. I'll maybe fetch the doctor tae him the morrow. A can and a nip please Jock, it's been a lang week!"

After a few more nips, Davy perked up a bit and for the first time in a while tried to strike up a conversation with the rest of the wee Sunday crowd. First, he tried Jock himself. But Jock was busy serving and cleaning glasses and watering down the whisky with a cheaper brand between times. Then, he tried Poachy Tam but Tam had been on the juice for near a week on the trot and was still bleezin from last night's lock-in at the Auld Inn at Gairnie. Finally, his gaze fixed on Sandy. The young lad was well into his cider and had his head in a book over by the window. Time for some sport thought Davy.

> He shambled over, drink in hand. "What you readin aboot today, Sandy?"
> The young man looked up and smiled. "It's an autobiography by a well-known cowboy film star. It's really interesting. One of his adopted kids was from Edinburgh and he's buried alongside his faithful horse Trigger. I've seen most of his films and, if you're into the traditional Hollywood Western Film genre he's a sort of cowboy super-hero."

Davy scratched his chin and looked a tiny bit puzzled. He'd never done well at school and words like genre and autobiography were not a regular part of his vocabulary.

> He struggled for a moment then blurted out "Ah right! Cowboys and Indians! Would that be about Roy Rogers and Tonto and the like? I've seen them on the telly. Widnae mind a fine big beast like thon Hi Ho Silver. Ye could tak him tae the likes o Clart Races and mak a few shillings. Now I'd be right fine wi aat! Aside fae thon big black eye-mask of course. Makes him look mair like a bandit."

> "You're maybe confusing The Lone Ranger with the Yodelling Cowboy" replied Davy. "And there were lots of horses in the films. In fact, I think Roy Rogers might have had as many as three Triggers. Or maybe more if you count the stunt doubles."

"Ah right" replied Davy "but why would he need three Triggers? Surely one would have been plenty enough for the man!"

"Well" began Sandy. "You'd need to understand first of all that Rogers appeared in over one hundred films plus numerous radio and TV productions. He lived well into his eighties. Horses don't make it that far. Hence the need for several replacements. The original Trigger in the films was actually named Golden Cloud and was born in San Diego.

He was often mistaken for a Tennessee Walking Horse but was more of a Heinz sort of fellow, his sire was a thoroughbred and his dam a Palomino just like the fictional Trigger in the original published stories.

Movie director William Witney, who directed Roy and Trigger in many of their movies, claimed a slightly different lineage, saying that his sire was a registered Palomino and his dam was a thoroughbred from a Cold Blood mare.

Horses other than Golden Cloud also portrayed Trigger over the years, but none of them were related to Golden Cloud. Two of the most prominent were palominos called Little Trigger and a horse called Trigger Junior who was a Tennessee Walking Horse listed as Allen's Gold Zephyr in the Tennessee Walking Horse registry.

The original Trigger remained a stallion his entire life but was never bred so he has no descendants. Rogers used both Trigger Junior and Allen's Golden Zephyr at stud for many years, and the horse named Triggerson that Roy's fellow actor Val Kilmer led on stage as a tribute to Rogers and his cowboy peers during the 1999 Academy Awards was reportedly a grandson of Trigger Junior.

Does that answer your question Davy?"

By this point, Davy's eyes had glazed over and it wasn't just down to the whisky and the pints. No wonder folk take their own life he thought. But he knew better than to upset the film buff even if he hadn't a clue what the mannie was on about. He downed what was left of his drinks and turned to Jock for more, but then had second thoughts.

Truth was, he'd heard enough about Hollywood horses to last him a lifetime. So, for once in his adult life, he made it home sober as a judge on a Sunday and as events were to prove, that maybe wasn't such a bad thing.

The doctor was called to attend to Davy's brother Robbie on the following day. It was around five o-clock in the afternoon when he made his way through the narrow hallway to the back bedroom of the cottage that Robbie and Davy had shared all their adult life. The sash-window was wide open but the smell in the room was unmistakeable and the place was filling up with flies.

"And how long has your brother been like this Mr Soutar?" asked Dr Morris.

"Weel doctor," replied Davy in his best Sunday voice "he's been nae weel for jist lang oer a week as far as I can mind. I've been leaving him his meals but since maybe last Monday, he's never touched a single drap o food nor drink doctor. And, as far as I can tell, he's just been sleepin awa and never even leaving the room. At least when I'm aroon that is! Truth is doctor, I'm at my wits end. He winna eat you see!"

"Mr Soutar" said the doctor gently "I'm afraid your brother's no longer with us. He's almost certainly been dead for some days as far as I can tell. I think I should make some phone-calls."

And with that, Jock's Shebeen at Clacharty lost a valued customer. But it never ended there. A few weeks later, the local bobby was moved to Inverness. They said it was part of a re-structuring exercise but folk in Clacharty soon found out that Dr Morris had reported the Secret Sunday Club to the authorities. When the police arrived, there was a scramble for the back door. They let most of the drinkers out but charged Jock with running an illegal drinking establishment under section something or other of the Licensing Act 1957.

Jock ended up in court and paid a hefty fine. Some said he was lucky to escape prison but that was maybe not the case. His business was in ruins though and he still owed the owner of Clacharty Motors for bankrolling auld Patterson's shop and Clacharty Pete had a reputation for collecting unpaid debt with a vengeance.

Just a few months after the court case there was a fire at the shop. The flat above was completely destroyed along with Jock and his wee mongrel Percy. They said it must have been a drunken chip pan blaze or a dropped cigarette in amongst the cushions of his settee. But locals maybe knew better.

The investigators thought it suspicious but nothing could be proved. It turned out that Pete the garage was sole beneficiary on the insurance and when he collected, the place was re-built and turned into flats. He'd gotten his money back and maybe even made a hefty profit on the deal.

For a time, until the licensing laws changed to allow Sunday opening, the Sunday drinkers made their way over to the grocer shop at Quorthies for a drink on the Sabbath. But when the rise of the big supermarkets put all the country shops out of business, the days of the secret Sunday clubs were clearly at an end. With the aid of a designated driver or maybe a taxi, anyone at all could have a legal drink in a pub on a Sunday in any week of the year. There was no need any more for subterfuge and the glory days of the back-shop boozers were lang awa.

Years later when he was on his death bed, Pete the garage was asked by the local minister about the fire at the shop.

> He simply replied, "well, it was a bit like deer stalking really. You need to cull the weaklings and instead of just killing them at the slaughterhouse, you simply kill them on the hill. If it was ony other bloody way around, nobody, aside fae the banks of course, would have made any money from it. And what in God's name would have been the sense in that meenister?"

13

THE QUINES THAT DID THE STRIP AT INVERMORRISAY
- 2nd October

The Palace of Westminster has its very own Strangers Bar and over at Invermorrisay, the toon hall Letting Committee had its very own Outsider Rates. If you were a local, you could simply pick up the keys from the hall keeper of an evening and open up the place yourself. Cubs and Scouts and

Brownies were charged just a few pounds for a four-hour hire and at closing time Akela or Baloo, or Bagheera, or Kaa, or Raksha, or Chil, or Hathi or maybe even Rama would call past the hall keeper's house and post the keys through the letter box in time for the amateur wrestling or the pipe band practice the next night. But if you were fae out of toon so to speak, things became a tad more complicated.

For starters, the charges were much higher for strangers. There was no obvious reason for it. But that was just the way it was in those days. In fact, it was the same for burials. If you hailed from out of town, you'd have to stump up extra to claim a spot in the local graveyard. Nobody knew why. It was just the way things had always been and nobody had a mind to change things.

As far as the toon hall was concerned, even big names like Andy Stewart and Chic Murray had to be vetted by the Letting Committee in case they were fly-by-nights and the powers that be charged them top-rates to use the facilities plus fifteen-percent of the door money. Most entertainers never came back to Invermorrisay ever again and that, despite several invites to join the hall committee, was why Dod declined the invitations.

In retaliation for the slight, one big-name performer even composed a revenge song about the quine that did the strip at Invermorrisay. It was all made up of course and in all probability the author of the ballad had never even heard about the night Snuffy Avril fae Torry performed at the venue. But it went down a storm nevertheless despite the fact that Snuffy, nor for that matter Big Nora the butcher's wife, never got a single mention in the song.

When Snuffy came to Invermorrisay, the tickets were all sold out in a couple of days and were soon changing hands in the public bar at the White Horse at a premium. The reputation of the lass had proceeded her and every young lad worth his salt was needing a front-row seat for what promised to be the performance of the year.

Now, Snuffy Avril was a widow woman. At least that's what she claimed. But in truth, she'd never been married in her life. Her agent had put her up to it. He claimed it put her in a better light and she went along with the charade since it seemed likely to attract a bigger turnout. Truth was, when she wasn't performing on stage, she made her money performing more intimate acts in the dimly lit back streets of Aberdeen. That was where she'd gained the nickname Snuffy. A hare lip had gone untreated in childhood and the resultant speech impediment rarely went unnoticed by her clients.

But she wasn't known as Snuffy Avril in her stripper guise and went by the stage name of Arabella Dickson which gave some clue as to the likely content of her stage act. And, in the lead up to the tattie holidays, Snuffy came to Invermorrisay along with JoJo the Jazz Singer and The Big Band plus a local warm-up act by a lad by the name of Danny Macpherson. Danny was a comedian and had a reputation for bawdy jokes which fitted in just fine with Snuffy's risqué act.

The format for the night was a light meal of French Fries along with Herbs de Provence Orange Roasted Chicken in a Basket served up with a guid few drinks to the accompaniment of an extended set by JoJo and The Big Band. Arabella was scheduled to perform at 10pm by which point, according to the agent, the audience would be well oiled and up for almost anything.

The lights in the hall were set low to enhance the mood and the bar in the foyer was doing a roaring trade the whole evening. The audience was mainly young men on a works night out from the local mill along with a smattering of tradesfolk along with their wives or girlfriends and by 9.30pm most folk were full of drink and looking forward to the big performance.

While the tables were being cleared, Andy the agent appeared on stage to announce the next act and on came Danny the warm-up man fae New Mordrach. Unusually, he was sober that night and the one-liners came out thick and fast. Many in the audience knew him from the local panto and that night he didn't disappoint. He rattled off a steady stream of smutty jokes and the drink-soaked punters lapped it all up. References to huge melons and enormous phalluses formed the basis of his act. But by that point in the evening, he could have gotten away with almost anything providing there was a grain of double-entendre involved and he kept up his relentless stream of smut for the contracted thirty minutes without so much as a heckle.

"Good evening, ladies and gentlemen! It's such a pleasure to be here in Invermorrisay tonight in front of such a wonderful audience. As the lady said to the bishop, thank you for having me tonight!"

"Now stop me if you've heard this one. How do you make your girlfriend scream during sex? Phone her up and tell her about it!"

"Why do women have orgasms? Just another reason to moan, really."

"Why does Santa Claus have such a big sack? He only comes but once a year. Boom boom!"

"How is a girlfriend like a laxative? They both irritate the shite out of you."

And finally.

"What did one butt cheek say to the other butt cheek? Together, we can stop this crap."

As he finished his warm up, a long drum roll introduced the big act of the evening. As the lights dimmed still further, Arabella Dickson marched stiffly onto the stage dressed for all the world like a female version of Danny La Rue on steroids.

To the accompaniment of the Big Band's rendering of The Stripper, her various layers of clothing landed up in a heap on the edge of the stage until only a feather boa, a pearl necklace and a pair of long white gloves remained onboard to tease the audience. Then, as the lights dimmed still further for a final drumroll Arabella Dickson exited stage left to be swiftly replaced by Andy the agent.

"Thank you all very, very, much! Thank you all! You've been such a wonderful audience!" he bellowed into the microphone.

"Please give a big hand to our acts tonight, JoJo and The Big Band, Danny Macpherson and the wonderful, incomparably magnificent Arabella Dickson! Thank you very, very, much ladies and gentlemen! It has been such a pleasure to perform for you all at Invermorrisay! Please enjoy the rest of your evening and have a safe journey home!"

There was a stunned silence from the audience. Nobody clapped. The big act had been on stage for only six or so minutes and she hadn't even taken all her clothes off! They were having none of it! A storm of half-empty beer cans and some fairly unrepeatable cat calls followed Andy into the wings and despite the dim onstage lighting, all three members of The Big Band could be seen scooping up their instruments and making a speedy exit before events took an even nastier turn.

The lights were still low when, fortified by a belly full of wine, Big Nora McHendry the local butcher's wife rose from her table and with a yell of "I can do much better than that! Just you watch me!" made her way up onto the front of the stage and, thrusting her chest skywards, kicked off her winter boots and began to rhythmically unzip the back of her dress.

Almost immediately, the crowd began chanting an improvised version of The Stripper and to the accompaniment of "Dah dah dah dah, dah dah dah dah, dah dah dah dah dah dah dah dah dah, dah dah dah dah dah, dah dah dah dah dah dah dah dah!" Nora began staggering around the stage performing her very own interpretation of the strip of the century.

Off came the dress and off came the blouse. And in much the same time it had taken Snuffy to get down to her feather boa and pearl necklace, Big Nora was down to her finest fancy bra and frilly knickers. It wasn't really a pretty sight but on that particular night in the town hall at Invermorrisay, nobody in the audience was much inclined to complain.

As the dah dah dah dah dah dah dah dah dahs reached a crescendo, and just as Big Nora was reaching round to unfasten her bra, it all became too much for the butcher. Grabbing his overcoat to preserve what was left of her modesty, he leaped on-stage and unceremoniously bundled his semi naked spouse into the wings.

It was the talk of the toon next day and for weeks afterwards, Big Nora was kept busy away from public gaze in the back shop of the butchers seeing to the sausages and the black puddings. It was only when the local minister gave a sermon on forgiveness that she ventured out in public to discover that, in her own small way, she'd become something of a local celebrity as the quine that had outstripped Snuffy Avril fae Torry.

As for Snuffy. She continued to perform her stripping routine occasionally throughout the Garioch and the Mearns but was soon back to her old ways at the harbour. By the time her looks snuck away she was, according to unkind folk at least, performing for the price of a bag of chips and a pickled onion.

Years later one local commentator was to record in print that "Aiberdeen fowk o a certin age wull a'm sure myn o Snuffy Avril, a prostitute fae Torry faa wis kent as the teethless hooer wi a hairt an a hare lip an, as legend his it, wid perform een o her services fer a fish supper. Noo a maan add, a'm nae spikkin fae personal experience as a wis only a sma geet in Snuffy's time. Eccentric? Maybe. Worthie? Maist definitely!"

An often-repeated tale concerns a vice squad raid on her wee flat in the Torry red light district.

> "When the police came knocking on the door she shouted out 'Whose there?'"
> "It's the police!" came the reply.
> "Well you'll have to effen wait your turn just like the rest o them!" shouted a busy Snuffy through the letterbox.

Another unlikely tale talks about her paying her takings from the previous night into her bank account the next morning. It came to £87-50.

> "Aye, aye, Avril," said the bank teller. "And who gave you the 50p then."
> "They a did." came the reply.

Kinder folk recalled that she had a habit of starting off a fine singsong on the Torry busses late at night and always had a sweetie for the local kids. But, by the time she made her way up the hill to the local cemetery, her flicker of fame as a stripper had been largely forgotten. In fact, by that point in time, most folk from the North East would give you a blank look if you brought up Snuffy's stripping career. After all, wasn't it Big Nora the butcher's wife who wis the real quine that did the strip at Invermorrisay?

WINTER

Caal, Weet Wiks

THE MART MANNIE'S REVENGE - 7th January

Dod was never one to believe in spirits although he did like a good dram on occasion. Sometimes he would meet in with a cousin whose mother was a seer. But after one too many serious weekend lunchtime sessions with his cousin Robbie fae Clacharty, he decided that it was maybe safer to observe the man's life from a distance and from hearsay. And, the stories weren't long in coming in.

The Souter croft at Clacharty was never the same after Alford. It was that difficult winter of 1979 and the diggers were busy on the deep-frozen farm roads. The cooncil had gied the fairmers in the Garioch each a snaa ploo for their tractors and had even promised some recompense for their time spent opening up the roads in winter. But a long blinding blizzard followed by some iron hard frosts had filled the roads with frozen drifts and made the ploos redundant. It was now a job for bright yellow JCB's with their big clanking iron buckets. Once the wind had dropped and the sun wis up, they smashed up the frozen drifts and coupit them ower the dykes to sit and melt till spring.

Winter aside, Robbie Souter had decided early on to train for the ministry. But due to this and that, he'd jist never gotten round to it. He was in his early thirties and had lived in the croft house at Clacharty since birth. The neighbours said that he had always been an ill-gattit child. Much given to tantrums he had driven his parents to despair and his brothers to wonder about his parentage. Sometimes he took out his rage on school pals. On one memorable occasion he beat up Beedie Bremner the Mart auctioneer's son for no reason little realising that years later, when the bubbling lad took on his father's sheen, he would exact his revenge.

Now, Robbie liked his whisky and in drink would attribute the stuff with spiritual qualities. This led him to drift effortlessly into bout drinking alongside a cohort of like-minded folk. And, often for days at a time, the croft would fill up wi a drouthy crowd and then empty again as the money and the whisky ran oot. By this time, Robbie was the man o the hoose. His dad had had a seizure at the Spring Show and died the same day. His auld mither would follow her man to the grave not long after. His brothers were busy with the ministry and there was nobody around to reign the man in.

At harvest time Robbie often worked for neighbours. On one such harvest, his pay was reserved for future use. The farmer at Clart, put the entire months earnings into a savings account for Robbie's future use and, after giving him pocket money, furnished Robbie wi "a pair or twa of fresh clean breeks" since the "airse wis clean hingin oot o the ones he wis wearing and we couldn't really countenance that. And we kent if we gied him the wages he wis due, he'd never have turned up the next day and we couldn't really countenance that either."

"Efter that we called him stainy-breeks which wis maybe unkind. But at least it gave us a laugh when we were yoking up in the morning and he didnae seem to mind."

But it was the disaster with the sheep that sparked the final death throes of the Souter croft. Just months after his dad died, Robbie had taken the March lambs to the Mart at Kinallarty for a special sale but had never brought either them nor the money back home.

It wasn't a long drive to Kinallarty but with one thing and another there were plenty of rest stops along the way. By the time Robbie and his pals Airchie Forbes and Raggidy Rab reached there they were bleezin. The sale began at two and the Souter Suffolks were duly unloaded in plenty of time and on their way to the holding pens and then into the ring.

As the auction began, Robbie slouched on the sale ring benches very much the worse for wear and very much out of pocket. He owed Bremner of Auchendroone plus a few others a hefty few drinks and Bremner's brother Beedie, the man he had beaten up all those years ago, was today's auctioneer.

The bidding was slow that day. And prices were at rock bottom. In a more sensible state of intoxication Robbie would have packed the Suffolks back into the float and headed back to the croft. But the whisky had had its way with him and he would have more of the dangerous stuff. After a few paltry bids it was obvious that the thing to do was to head home and try again another day. But when the auctioneer quite correctly asked "Are we selling today, Mr Souter? Or do you wish to withdraw your beasts from the sale?" the whisky won the day and the entire years flock of mutton went for buttons.

"Aye, sell the buggers!" he cried out and the deed was duly done.
"Going once, twice and gone to Bremner of Auchendroone." said Beedie with more than a hint of a smile on his face.

Not everyone laughed, but a good few sniggered at the spectacle of the drunken Robbie selling off the family siller for sic a chape-John price and to a Bremner as well. But only a very few had ony inkling that the mart mannie had maybe gotten his revenge for that sair beating all those years ago.

After the old lady died things changed again. There was little in the estate apart from the croft house and a few spindly ewes well past their best and a few dozen acres of scrubby croft land infested with ragwort and nettles. The land was sold off piecemeal for houses and for a while at least the cash rolled steadily in and things in the world of Robbie stumbled on. Eventually though, Robbie ran out of funds. He took in a bunch of ne'er do well lodgers in an effort to keep body and spirit alive.

In the course of that most severe of winters in 1986, when the temperature in Centigrade plummeted to minus 27 degrees in neighbouring Braemar he faced a stark choice. Either heat the house or buy whisky. Being a resourceful sort of lad, he found a middle way. First, he burned the doors for heating, then the floorboards went. The stairs were next which made life difficult in the auld hoose. Then the pipes froze and things got even more difficult.

Using the paltry income from his bunch of ne'er do well lodgers he bought whisky. And then mair whisky. Then much mair o the same. By the March, the house was just a shell and the lodgers had gone elsewhere looking for an easier place to stay. It was time for Robbie to move on and it was time for a big lifestyle change. Almost as easily as he had adopted whisky as a way of life, he stopped drinking and studied for the ministry. But there was one final, and almost fatal twist in the Robbie saga.

Now, Robbie kept dogs which lived outside in the lean to. One day in a January blizzard, a cross collie called Zak broke out and bit the plumber's daughter. Mr Jopps the plumber, duly broke out his shotgun, went round to the croft and shot the dog. He then threatened to shoot Robbie as well. The police were called.

At the court case, Sheriff Smith advised the plumber that the only reason he was not imposing a prison sentence was due to the unique nature of the offence.

> "Were it not for the fact that the shotgun was broken when you threatened the plaintiff, I would have no choice but to send you to jail. However, I have heard from counsel that you merely intended to shoot the dog and not the unwitting owner of the animal."
> "Thank you, your honour." replied counsel for Mr Jopps.
> "I shall impose a severe fine for the offence of discharging a firearm in a public place and I warn you not to test this court again!" said the Sheriff.
> "Thank you, your honour." replied counsel for Mr Jopps.

A more enlightened Sheriff might have sent the joiner to jail for shooting the dog. But Sheriff Smith was old school and well past his sell by date. He retired soon after the case and in his final weeks on the bench liked to entertain his courtroom with harum-scarum tales of his wartime days as a military dispatch rider in the Libyan desert.

The Souter croft house still stands and looks just as tummle-doon as it did when Robbie left. The garden space is pretty much all that's left of the land and the site will no doubt soon be made into splendid houses for folk to do with the oil and the bank will maybe get a portion back of what it's owed as weel. As for Robbie? He became known locally as the Whiskey Priest after he eventually qualified for the ministry. But, as far as anyone knew, he never preached due to his continuing love affair with the bottle.

15

THE TERMINATOR – 12th December

Once a month on his Friday off, Dod drank at the Kittybrewster Railway Club in Aberdeen. It was there he met in with an elderly lad named Josh who claimed to be known in railway circles as The Terminator.

Josh McBride had been an engine driver just at the end of steam and had converted to diesel just a few years before his retirement. Railwaymen throughout the North East of Scotland, he said, knew him affectionately as The

Terminator due to the number of rail suicides he'd experienced in his engine driving career. He'd begun his working life in a shunting yard at Kirkintilloch and had a lucky break when he got the chance to make fireman on the steam trains. Driving came next and he never looked back.

"If you took time to think about it" said Josh, "you'd maybe never get out of bed in the morning to go off to your work. Some drivers never get over the first incident but most never experience it first-hand. Luck of the draw I suppose and I've just been especially unlucky.

Sometimes there can be wee obstacles on the track like a broken branch or a maybe a sheep and you have to watch your way and slow down a bit in the bad weather. You get used to dead animals on the line. You might hit a deer or a farmer's sheep on a rare occasion but when it comes to humans, well that's something quite different if you ask me.

The track maintenance guys generally carried a sack for the dead deer. If it's a fresh kill they maybe bag the haunch and share out the best bits amongst the gangers. But when it comes to the humans, they have to step aside and let the emergency services deal with the mess. And, believe me, it can be a right mess. I should know. I experienced it eight times in my driving career."

"Eight!" exclaimed Dod. "How on earth did you cope with that?"

Josh lit another cigarillo before continuing.

"Well, the first one I killed was a wee lass over at Kirkintilloch. That was before I moved to the North East of course. She couldn't have been more than fifteen and they said it was deliberate. Maybe trouble at home or something. I never really knew. Then there was that jumper that leapt off the footbridge near Glasgow Central. I watched him fall but there was nothing I could do apart from slam on the brakes. When we eventually came to a stop, there was nothing much left of him. The entire train had rolled over his body. It was quite a mess. He'd been homeless apparently and had maybe just had enough.

The early ones were quite a shock but you soon get over it and you think that it won't, can't, happen again. But, in my case it kept on happening and after the fourth, a farm lad near Drinnies, I just accepted it as a hazard of the job. Plus-side was you got time off to attend the inquest. Downside was all the interviews and the forms to fill in."

As the drinks went in, the tales of blood and gore just kept on coming.

"Then there was that old guy on the bend near the brickworks at Invermorrisay. Now that was an odd one. They reckoned he'd been thinking about ending it for ages. Various folk had spotted him in the bushes alongside the line over the course of a few days but nobody had thought anything of it. Perhaps they imagined he was out snaring rabbits or bird spotting. Anyway, after he went out on the line, they found a wee tent and a pile of vodka empties in behind a trackside shed so he'd not just been checking out the wildlife. They had to scrape him off the track. But by that time, I was away over in Aberdeen."

"Did you not stop to see what had happened?" said Dod.

"It wasn't a hit and run if that's what you're thinking!" Said Josh indignantly. "It's just that you don't always know you've hit someone. They usually jump at the last second and you might not see them. Out of my eight, I only knew about six of them at the actual time. It sometimes wasn't until hours later that I would get told that it must have been my train that was involved and even then, you can never really be completely certain. I mean, my final score might actually have been much higher if you think about it."

By this point in the afternoon, Dod decided that he'd maybe downed enough drink and heard enough gory railway chat to last him a lifetime. Finishing up his fourth pint, he made his excuses and headed off for the teatime Bluebird bus back to Invermorrisay and home.

The next month when he went to the club, there was no sign of Josh. Nor the next or the next. In fact, he never met up with the man again and whenever he enquired after him, no one had ever heard of him. The bar staff had no recollection of him and none of the regulars appeared to have any inkling. In fact, it seemed that Josh the Terminator had simply never existed and that the mid- December drinking session had maybe just been a hallucination.

Even the notion that a single train driver could be unfortunate enough to encounter eight suicides in a career seemed far-fetched. When he re-told the tale, Dod was greeted with disbelief and even a measure of ridicule.

"Nobody could be that unlucky," was the typical response. "Are you sure you weren't on the wacky baccy Mr King?"

But, Dod remained convinced that, even if the man's tale was partly fiction, there might be some element of truth in it all. He'd met up with him in a railway social club after all. And it was a thing that happened on the railway from time to time. There were even blackspots, on bends and at bridges, where he was aware that suicides had occurred more than once. And, often as not, the details of what had happened were never fully written up in the press from fear of upsetting relatives or encouraging copy-cats. But over the years, the Josh McBride episode continued to niggle away, especially when Dod had occasion to visit the Kittybrewster Railway Club in Aberdeen.

Now, one of the duties of a county librarian is to take charge of the local studies collection. And, with Invermorrisay being a railway town, the library shelves held a decent pile of books and historical documents about the history of the local railway repair works and the Beeching Cuts and all things to do with the permanent way since way back in Victorian times.

One day, an information request came in from a reporter at the Invermorrisay Herald & Post. They were working up a feature story about a local lad whose great uncle had moved up from Glasgow to be a train driver just after the end of the First World War and could Dod maybe see if the library held any records about the man. The desk clerk had taken the phone call and passed Dod a note with all the details.

"Josh Henry McBride (1892-1921). Railway engine driver born Shettleston, Glasgow. Buried Cluny Hill Cemetery, Forres. Latterly resident in Forres. Thought to have committed suicide by train 12th December 1921 near Forres Railway Station."

Intrigued, Dod took the note over to the newspaper archives. And there, improbably and in the deepest depths of the library micro-fiche reels for December 1921 was a brief but graphic account of the event that led to the death of the man he had apparently met in person just a year or so ago in the Railway Club in Aberdeen.

"A TRAGIC AND UNFORTUNATE DEATH ON THE RAILWAY LINE AT FORRES - December 12th 1921

A tragic event occurred last Tuesday near Forres when the Aberdeen bound passenger train from Inverness collided with a pedestrian straying on the track near the viaduct at Findhorn. The South bound steam train had just emerged at speed onto the long straight leading to the station at Forres and had begun slowing down when, without any warning, a Mr J.H. McBride, a former engine driver of that town appeared suddenly on the track. There was little that the train engineer or the duty fireman could do to prevent the tragedy and Mr McBride is thought to have been killed instantaneously when the locomotive's wheels passed over his body. Police and a local surgeon attended the scene and the remains were conveyed by ambulance to the local mortuary prior to burial at a later date by the grieving widow, Mrs Elizabeth Morag McBride of Elgin town.

No fault whatsoever can be attributed to the engineer and it is thought that the unfortunate victim may have deliberately placed himself in mortal danger whilst being of unsound mind due to a series of similar events of this nature having occurred in the course of his own duties as a railway engineer.

An inquest into the accidental death will be held Tuesday next at Inverness Sheriff Court House."

After passing on the details to the Herald reporter, Dod headed over the road to the Bakers Arms for an extended liquid lunch during which he vowed never to breath a wird aboot his meet-up with The Terminator ever again.

16

THE WRANG LUM – 24th December

In Dod's day, the bulk of fire stations in rural Scotland were manned by part-time fire-fighters. It just wouldn't have been affordable to man them full-time. They were called retained firefighters and in exchange for a few pounds and a shiny new fireproof uniform were expected to leap oot of bed at a moment's notice whenever the alarm went off at the fire station. One of Dod's neighbours had spent time as a retained fireman in Buchan. And over a winter dram, he told Dod aboot the big disaster over at Firtybogs.

On a scale from one to ten, the Christmas blaze at Firtybogs was a pretty minor affair. In fact, if left completely alone, the fire in the lum would have simply fizzled out and no-one aside fae the occupants of the affected part of the row of farm cottages would have been ony the wiser. On a scale of one to ten, the blaze scored around the level two mark. But come what may, an emergency is an emergency and Buchan's finest were summoned oot on Christmas Eve to tackle the tiny conflagration.

Now, Firtybogs is jist doon the road from the Bloo Toon jist aff the road between Maud and Old Deer. A ferm toon in the older days the place is just a tiny spot on the map and you could swing by it in less than half a second. In fact, most folk do.

Neeps and sheep and kail were the main thing there alongside a few dozen laying hens and maybe a grunter if they had a mind for killing and salting it. Aside from a dubby track and a tummle-doon roadside sign, there wis nothing much remarkable about the place. In fact, if you were to take a photograph, nobody except the nearest neighbours and the postie would have the slightest idea where in the world the place was. It wis that anonymous you see.

The emergency call came in to Peterhead Police Station at half-past two in the morning just as Santa was doing his rounds. Firtybogs had a chimney fire and could the Maud volunteers maybe take the shout. Well, the answer was a resounding yes and, before anyone could even take sae much as a pee, twa pumps and a higgledy-piggledy squad of local volunteers headed out to see what could be done. There were butchers and joiners and bankers and roofers among the crew and, by the time they reached the road end at the seat of the blaze, they were all dressed up in their fire-brigade gear and raring tae go and sort it all out.

It was a dirty fire. The chimney heid atop the shared cottar hoose roof, was well ablaze and sparks were fair loupin out the lum. But the lad in charge could see that it was just a wee emergency. It would maybe burn itself out with no real danger to man nor beast. Maybe someone was burning out the soot. Or maybe the greasy wrappings from a fish supper had fed the flames. No matter. This was a training opportunity. And, despite the time of year, it was one not to be missed.

The new lad on the job was Angus Smart fae Aikey. He'd done all the training but had never actually attended a proper fire. So, in a kind of way, it was a Nazareth moment for the young lad. A big Fire Brigade ladder was put up against the gable end and young Angus grabbed the end of the hose and clambered up the roof. By the time he reached the ridge, the flames had quietened down a bit to be replaced by a thick black pall of smoke. There wis a shout fae down below. "Are you ready?"

"Aye, turn it on," came the excited reply.

Over the next five or so minutes, the young fire fighter poured the water fae the hose into the chimney pot until at last the fire, or whit wis left of it, gave up and fizzled oot. Then a cry went up fae doon below.

"You've stuck it doon the wrang bliddy lum ye blin feel!"

As Angus climbed back doon tae earth, there was a right hullabaloo going on below. Next door's front door lay wide open and a greetin quine wis standing by the gate in the yard clutching a bubbly-bairn and a cage containing a pair of sooty budgerigars. All four of them were completely drookit. But even worse was what was inside the cottage.

It looked as though a biblical flood had sped its way doon the stairs and into the living room and the place wis full of sticky soot fae the upstairs chimney in the front bedroom. The Santa socks above the fireplace had somehow survived. But the pile of presents underneath the tree had seen better days and the carpets were completely ruined.

There wis clearly a big apology to be made and compensation was quickly offered. But Buchan's finest took an affa hard ribbing for the nicht they tried tae droon Santa Claus.

As for next door's lum fire at number two? It had jist burned itself oot on its own nae bather at aa. In fact, if it wisna for all the fuss, and all the blue lights and the loud shouting and the sirens and the bubbly-bairn, the neighbours next door would have probably been none the wiser aboot the fire in their lum.

17

ARWYN'S CARAVAN – 25th January

The old mannie in the caravan had clearly seen some better days and each
fortnight when the library van called past to deliver his books, the extent of his
decline became more and more obvious to the staff.

Arwyn Davies had been a regular at the library for several years but when
his health began to decline the visits became rarer until eventually, he would
phone in his book order and hobble down the field to meet the van at the

crossroads at the appointed time. When even that became difficult, the driver would park at the at the foot of the short track that led up through the field below the caravan and deliver the books personally. On different days, the fish van and the grocer's van and the baker's van would follow suit and for that final couple of years the old man clung on to his independence and his eccentricities.

In the days when he had been more able, Arwyn's library visits would usually coincide with a trip to the local shops and Dod tended to look forward to a brief chat with the man. At the very least these weekly visits heralded a break from the drudgery of the issuing desk or the stacking of shelves full of pulp fiction and middling novels. And at its best, you could have a decent discussion about local politics or standing stones or astrology or just about any topic under the sun.

By all accounts, Arwyn had arrived in the area in around 1984 from Cardiff and had seemingly worked for a while in the brewing industry before becoming a rural milkman. The work was on a self-employed basis and it suited his lifestyle perfectly.

> "You get the roads and the countryside pretty much to yourself until maybe eight-o-clock in the morning and, most days, you're finished by midday with the rest of the day ahead of you," he would tell folk. "Fridays are completely different though. You have to do the morning round and then head back out in the early evening to collect the dues then get up again at four to start the Saturday deliveries."

In his time off from the milk, he could sometimes be seen, Hasselblad in hand, exploring and photographing the multitude of free museums full of standing stones and Pictish remains which lay scattered all around the shire and rumour had it that he was busy writing a book about them but no one really knew when, if ever, it would be published.

Truth was, Arwyn had only ever published one short article and that was in a local glossy magazine. But that didn't really matter. The label as a writer gave him credibility and provided him access to anyone and to any place around the Garioch and far beyond. And that suited the man very well. He liked the freedom that the cover story gave him and he soon blended into the local community as an acceptable and respected eccentric.

By and by though, Arwyn's fortunes declined. The buying habits of country folk had changed and the demand for daily milk deliveries declined. Most folk in the countryside now had access to cars and were much more inclined to do a big weekly shop at the supermarkets and would, like as not, stock up with dairy products from the food cathedrals. The market for door-step deliveries shrank and the days of the country milkie were numbered. There came a point where the cost of the diesel and the hire of the milk float from the dairy left little in the pocket of the roundsmen and, one by one, the breed disappeared over the horizon to find new employment wherever they could.

In Arwyn's case, he was reaching late middle-age and had no intention of re-joining the rat race. His stint in the brewing industry had left him cold.

"At least the Germans and the Belgians have gotten it right!" he would tell friends. "They only use yeast and hops and water to brew their beer. Not like it is here where there's one fancy chemical to make it froth, another to make it fizzy and yet another to make it less frothy when you pour the stuff into a glass! Pure poison if you ask me! Pure poison!"

When asked what he planned to do for a living after the milk delivery career, he would refer to the book he had in preparation and if pressed, would reveal that it was nearly complete and almost ready to submit to a publisher. In the meantime, he was happy to survive on savings and, in a bid to cut down on expenses, he moved from his damp rented cottage on the edge of Kinallarty to an old damp caravan at Potts of Clatt Castle for a peppercorn rent. The arrangement between the Welshman and the estate owner involved the renovation of an adjoining farm house but lack of funds meant that the project never even got as far as the planning stage. The local laird was to recall years later that he knew in his heart of hearts that the likelihood of the renovation taking place was slim but that he had a soft spot for the eccentric Arwyn.

In the years following the move to the caravan, the Welshman's reputation as an astrologer attracted a following and he made a living of sorts from producing birth charts and running workshops. For a few pounds he would teach you what Russell Grant was on about. For a few pounds more, he would demystify Mystic Meg.

He supplemented the astrology with a kitchen garden and some laying hens and could turn his hand to car repairs as and when his aging campervan needed a new set of spark plugs or an urgent exhaust repair. But all the while, he was accumulating cats. Lots of cats!

It had started with a single stray. Then another stray appeared but pregnant this time. Then a set of kittens then another set of kittens, but inbred this time. And so it went on. Within a year of his move to the caravan there were ten dependant moggies roaming around the place as if they owned it and were paying the rent. An old dining-room table propped up beside an open window provided access day and night and allowed the semi feral beasties free reign around the place. The number would go up on occasion to as much as twenty. Then as cat flu and inbreeding and other feline ailments grabbed a hold, they would settle at a steady nine or ten for a bit before skyrocketing yet again.

By the time Arwyn was in his terminal decline the cats had pretty much taken over his living space. If, like his astrology clients or his fast-dwindling group of friends, folk were brave enough to visit they would find themselves surrounded by a swarm of sneezing moggies and all the paraphernalia that went with the territory. Cat bowls and litter trays full of stinky earth were strewn around the place and, often as not, a rotting roadkill rabbit or a flattened badger collected by a sympathetic neighbour would be lying outside the caravan door for consumption by the peelie-wally horde. The carpets and the seats were sticky from the years of neglect and, like as not, any casual visitor would head home after the visit for a well needed shower and a change of clothes.

When the old man finally died and the cats had been humanely dealt with, the laird was faced with the problem of what to do with his possessions and what to do with the remains of the dilapidated caravan. There were no relatives on the horizon so what was salvageable was carted off in boxes to be stored in a shed over at the big house. A local scrappy agreed to cart off the campervan for spares and the laird's handyman stripped the caravan in preparation for burning. It was then that the factor found the safe.

It was one of those small green cast-iron jobs normally found in pubs or grocers. There were two large keyholes next to the handle alongside a shiny brass plaque proclaiming 'Chubb of Manchester England and Appointed by Royal Warrant'. It sat partially buried under a huge pile of mouldy clothing in a cupboard next to the bed. A brief search revealed the safe keys taped to the underside of the bedside drawer.

The scrappy offered to dispose of the safe free of charge as part of the clear up. But on opening the big cast iron door, the factor felt duty bound to call the laird who called the police. For inside the safe lay a large bank bag full of bundled cash plus what looked very much like a First War era service revolver. A second, smaller, bag held a bright yellow gold ingot which on later inspection proved to bear the refiner's mark and the serial number of a gold bar stolen in the 1983 Brink's-Mat bullion heist. The police immediately began an investigation, but failed to find any link between the big Welshman and the robbery.

The mystery was further compounded when the local authority stepped in to arrange for the cremation of Arwyn's remains. No one had come forward to claim the body and nobody who knew him could point to any living relatives. And when officials tried to register the death, the Registrar could find no record of the man. He quite simply didn't officially exist. There was no record of his birth or marriage and no National Insurance Number existed in the name of Arwyn Davies. His driving licence proved to be a clever fake and the passport he had used to open his bank account turned out to be a forgery.

The Inland Revenue had no file on him. He'd made a thing about never paying tax.

> "If you give the buggers your hard-earned money, they'll just spend it on guns and bombs!" he would tell friends. "Better not to earn enough to pay it in the first place."

And there were no medical records dating from before he'd arrived in the area in 1985. Fingerprints and dental records revealed absolutely nothing and the serial number on the gun had been carefully filed off. It was all a bit of a mystery and the folk who thought that they had known Arwyn had to accept that they really hadn't really known much about him at all.

Eventually the body of the man who claimed to be Arwyn Davies was released by the coroner for cremation by the council. His real identity was never established and the Brink's-Mat Robbery link remains a mystery to this day.

There were various theories about the source of Arwyn's hidden wealth. Some folk said he must have been a money launderer. Others thought he might have been in on the robbery from the start and had chosen anonymity in witness protection to avoid a hefty jail sentence. Still others dismissed the story out of hand. Why would a rich robber end his days as a pauper in a tummle-doon cat infested caravan after all?

As for Dod, he liked to imagine that the elusive Mr Davies from Wales was in fact the real Charles Calthrop from the Forsyth novel. But the jury is still out on that theory.

SPRING

Caal an Wairmer Weet Wiks

18

THE KEITH BAG SHOP – 25th March

Dod was never much one for the kirk. He only attended church for weddings and funerals as a rule. But he had an ear for clerical gossip and the antics of one particular son of the manse soon caught his attention.

There was a new minister over at Gairnie. After the Doddy Mutch eulogy affair, the Right Reverend Evered was never seen again and the Right Reverend Ranald McRobert from Edinburgh took up the vacant post. He had a wife and a pair of teenage boys and had arrived in late March to live in the big barn of a manse opposite the graveyard. It was a cold and drafty sort of place even in summer, and the older son soon took off to be a car salesman in Glasgow. That left young Jamie to cope as best he could without his sibling in what were completely unfamiliar surroundings for a city boy.

Now, the young lad had never really fitted in to parish life. Even in his native Edinburgh, the interminable routine of church services and all the duties of the manse had never quite appealed to him. But he was at heart a solitary lad and the slower pace of the countryside gradually grew on him. On top of all of that, he had a puckle of psychiatric problems and sometimes believed he was Jesus.

He soon fell in with a bunch of art school types who rented a tummle-doon row of cottar houses over at Clart and most days, rain or shine throughout that first spring and summer, he could be seen riding over the hill to Clart on his shiny red and cream Honda moped.

There was a craft potter in one cottage working intensely on his degree piece. Another housed a final year teacher in training and the third was occupied, just now and then, by a drug addicted depressive artist working his way slowly through his blue period. All in all though, it was a welcoming sort of space and Jamie soon found that he could come and go as he pleased and that suited him just fine.

After a few weeks, the artist lad offered Jamie the use of his spare room to store his stuff. He'd noticed that the rack on the young lad's moped was habitually piled high with part filled plastic shopping bags and was concerned that the ever-growing pile of stuff on the back of the bike might overwhelm the machine and cause an accident. A grateful Jamie happily accepted the offer and immediately began to fill the tiny room with bags.

At first, these were thin polyethylene single-use shopping bags of the type you'd maybe get at the likes of Sainsburys or Asda. But over the next few weeks Jamie began to appear with entire moped loads of those ex-army canvas shoulder bags that working folk used to use for their pieces at lunchtime.

You know the sort of thing. About the size of a Post Office telephone directory with a long-brass-buckled shoulder strap stitched onto the sides and a big buckle-down flap to keep the sarnies dry and stop the coffee flask from falling out and smashing on the ground.

There were several variations in colour. Khaki for the army and light blue for the RAF. Grey was maybe for the navy. But they were all made from the same sturdy military grade canvas. And, aside from the colour, they were all exactly the same. Produced in their tens of millions in the war, they had been designed to hold, not a piece box or a Thermos, but an anti-gas device commonly known as a Military Grade Respirator or gas mask.

The government of the day officially retained ownership of the devices and demanded their return after the war had ended. But few bothered to return either the masks or the shoulder bags. In any case, the Ministry of Supply had vast warehouses full of unissued bags and that led to a bonanza for military surplus dealers all across Europe. For just a few shillings you too could be the proud owner of a Military Grade Respirator Bag Mk3 in any colour you wanted as long as it was in khaki or grey or light blue.

At first, nobody at the cottages took much notice of Jamie's daily deliveries of gas mask bags. But, as the room began to fill, and the smell of damp canvas began to permeate the place and folk began to wonder what he was up to. Where was Jamie getting these from? And what on earth was inside the bags?

But, there was a certain civility amongst the Clart students and no one volunteered to investigate what was in essence none of their business. Jamie had the use of the room and that was that. End of story. Whatever he did with the space was up to him and him alone. As for the smell. The place was already damp as a rule and only really dried out at the height of summer and the depressive artist secretly liked the dank atmosphere since it added to his melancholy. And wasn't that a good thing for his art?

By the end of May, the tiny room was stuffed full almost to the ceiling and Jamie began to fill the old tool shed beside the outside toilet. There was one communal privy for all three cottar houses but no one had much interest in the old shed. The roof leaked like a sieve and the big wooden door and its broad lintel had ended up as kindling the previous Christmas. But, the lack of a door did expose the bag collection to public gaze and folk again began to wonder.

By this time, the bag collector's wee red moped was quite the worse for wear. Winter road salt had pitted the chrome and the brightly painted petrol tank had long lost its shine. On top of that, Jamie had mislaid the petrol cap and replaced it with a piece of cloth. The springs had pretty much gone due to rust and the bumpy roads and worst of all, the engine was completely seized due to lack of oil. But the clutch still worked and Jamie took to pushing his bike to the cottages then back up the hill to the manse each day and the piles of canvas bags just kept on getting higher.

By now, the group of students were calling them 'Jamie Bags' and they were getting more and curious as to where Jamie was getting the things and what on God's earth he was up to.

Come the end of Spring the shed was full to bursting and Jamie had started a new heap in the old hen shed behind the privy. This was too much and a tenants meeting was hastily convened to sort out what to do. No one in the group wanted to upset the young lad. They'd kind of gotton fond of both him and his unusual ways and in any case the lease was up come for renewal at the end of term and none of them had a mind to stay on. A group decision was made to just tolerate the situation for the remaining weeks of the tenancy and to discover, if at all possible, what on earth Jamie was up to. The landlord, a businessman from Holland, could sort out the mess after they had gone and, in any case, there was a planning application to tear the entire place down to make way for a housing development for wealthy oil folk. So, the bulldozers could likely make short work of the Jamie Bag collection.

Josh, the melancholic artist, was chosen to do the investigating. It was he after all who had created the problem in the first place. If he'd policed the spare room in the early days, the matter could have been resolved without a fuss months ago. So, the melancholic Josh was on hand the next day when Jamie arrived with his bike load of bags.

"Hi Jamie! Fine day and how are you today?" bellowed Josh.
"Same as always," replied Jamie "busy as usual, so much to do. Don't know if I'll ever finish to be honest. There's loads more up there and they all need filling. I'll maybe need more help soon as well."

This was a good start thought Josh. In fact, it was probably the longest conversation the pair had had in several weeks. They'd mainly just gotton on with their separate things. Josh with his disturbingly depressive paintings and Jamie with his disturbingly obsessive bag collecting.

"What sort of help?" asked Josh.
"Oh, I've stopped my medication again. What do doctors know after all?" came the reply. "And I can only find enough empty crisp packets to

fill a couple of bags each day. It's difficult work you know. And it'll just get harder in summer when I can't always be a good Jesus."

This was something of a shock and not quite the answer he'd been expecting. But Josh carried on regardless more determined than ever to get to the bottom of the 'Jamie Bag' mystery. Over the next hour or so and over numerous cups of strong Nescafe, Josh gently coaxed the story out of Jamie.

The bags needed filling with empty crisp packets because Jamie had invented a secret process to re-manufacture them into shoe leather. It was just that he'd underestimated the sheer volume of crisp packets needed to start off the process. Hence the bags. They were needed to store the packets until he had enough to make the first twelve pairs after which the whole process would work automatically.

"Why twelve?" asked Josh.

"Well one for each disciple of course!" came the reply. "Isn't it obvious?"

As for the source of the bags? That turned out to be a haberdashery in Keith. Alongside an extensive line in fabric and buttons the owners, a Mr and Mrs Black from Huntly maintained a back shop stuffed full of army surplus with a big emphasis on the sort of things that farm folk and country folk might want. The gas mask bags had proved a big hit and much of that was down to regular visits from Jamie.

On mart days he would hitch a lift on a cattle-float up to Keith, buy up as many bags as he could carry, then hitch a float lift back home with his sack load of prizes. As often as not the returning drivers would take him right by his door at the manse and sometimes even share a fancy piece on the way down through the glens. Nobody appeared to have questioned what he was up to. He was just seen as a harmless oddity and was accepted for what he was.

Josh duly reported back to the group and the consensus was to let sleeping dogs lie. They would all be moving out soon and the landlord could maybe deal with the bag infestation. Meantime, they would just have to go along with the young lad's obsessive behaviour as if it was normal.

A month or so after the lease at Clart was up, Josh bumped into Jamie's older brother Pete in a pub at Auchalarty. When he asked after Jamie, Pete was at first hesitant. But after a bit of prodding and probing, he revealed that his wee brother had ended up back in a locked ward in an Edinburgh hospital after an unfortunate episode on Arthur's Seat.

"He'd been off his medication for weeks," said Pete "and just like the last time and the time before that, he'd become delusional. On this occasion he was reported to the police by a group of Japanese tourists hiking near the crags overlooking Holyrood. He'd been up there soaking wet and preaching to hill walkers for several days and when the police found him, he was raving on about crisp packets and soles for the disciple's shoes to help them spread the word of Jesus. He's much better now that he's had treatment but it'll probably happen again sometime soon."

A year or so later, a colleague at the library drew Dod's attention to a report on the front page of an Edinburgh newspaper. It was about a tragedy involving a twenty-something year old man found dead below the cliffs at Salisbury Crags. His name was Jamie McRobert. Seemingly the minister's lad fae Gairnie Manse had finally ascended unto heaven.

19

PIGGIE GOT HIM – 29th March

In early spring, just before the rush of new vegetation arrived to obscure the view over the Garioch countryside, Dod often took a Sunday afternoon stroll up through the forestry plantation at Old Foggie Woods then on up to the viewpoint at Little Nether Tap. From there you could get a clear view of the peaks of Ben Aucherie and you could even make out the shattered roof of the old abandoned piggery at Clart that had caused all the fuss back in 1957.

The narrow muddy path back down the hill took him past the stone circle on the roadside below Auchalarty and then back round the base of the hill to the tiny car park at Quarthies.

It was maybe a ninety-minute circular walk. Sixty if you didn't pause for breath or sandwiches along the way and he'd been this way many times before. But, on this particular occasion he made a detour past the old railway halt at Drinnies then over the wee humpy brig that spanned the Runcie Burn and up through the old graveyard at Mordrach. It was here that he stumbled upon Heinrich Winkler's grave.

He knew the man from the library and had heard that he'd been moved into the care home over at Clart a year or so ago suffering from some kind of difficult dementia. And here he was lying at peace in his adopted land alongside his baby daughter, surrounded by a clutch of dead farmers and a scattering of local nobility a thousand miles or more from his native Leipzig. There was no sign of his wife Elma on the headstone though. But that was to be expected. And no grave for little Willy either, only a little inscription on the gravestone about the missing child.

A tall blond man with striking blue eyes, Heinrich had arrived in Invermorrisay towards the end of 1944. But not through choice. He'd been in several British POW camps before landing up in Scotland and the authorities had initially classified him as a committed National Socialist and an ardent supporter of Hitler.

Like many Germans of the time, he'd graduated from the Hitler Youth to the SS and had the blood group tattoo on his arm to prove it. But, like many in his situation, he soon realised that downplaying his right-wing views was likely to lead to an easier life. So, over the course his first few months in captivity his political classification changed from black belligerent to grey and then to white. This allowed a degree of fraternisation with the locals and he soon found himself out on work parties cutting timber or gathering in the harvest in the woods and in the fields of the North East for a small amount of pay.

By the late 1940s, all but a few of the camps had emptied or been repurposed as re-settlement facilities for soldiers and refugees whose former homes in the East of Germany were now under Soviet control.

The guard towers stood empty and any prison gates that still remained lay wide open and largely unmanned. By this time Heinrich had secured himself full-time employment on a local farm. A tiny farmworkers cottage came with the job and it wasn't long before Heinrich settled into the local community. He'd met in with a local lass at the dancing and they were soon married, happy and expecting. It was after the birth of their second child, a blonde blue-eyed daughter, that everything went horribly wrong.

Heinrich had moved into town by this time and had secured a well-paid job at the local engineering company as a turner. At the interview, he'd been asked about his service background and his ability to work a lathe. He'd been frank about the war service.

> "Everybody of my age in Germany at that time was blinded by Hitler and his big promises. That was just the way it was. You did what was expected of you. Even your parents and your teachers would tell you so. There was no way to think otherwise. In fact, you'd have been a fool to go against the system," he told the interviewer.
>
> "And once you were in the army, you did exactly as you were told to do. Otherwise, they would punish you severely. Maybe even they would shoot you! Because that did happen in many cases. I kid you not and I have seen this with my own eyes!
>
> But I expect it was the same for the British and also for the Americans. And I served my time in the prisoner camps without any blemish whatsoever on my records as you can plainly see from my release papers! I just got on with the job of being a prisoner and never caused any trouble. What else was I supposed to do?"

The lad on the other side of the desk nodded in agreement. He'd been captured in the desert by the Italians and, like Heinrich, had spent years in the camps before being repatriated at the end of the war. The pair would later become friends if only for the common experience.

> "And can you work machinery?" asked the interviewer. "By that I mean drills and lathes and engineering hand tools. Can you read a drawing? Can you work accurately and to tolerances?"

> "Ah! Yes, yes!" replied Heinrich. "I can do that well enough. We were taught how to use metal working tools and machines in High School you see. The only difference is the measurements. You see, we were working in units of ten, unlike the British and the Americans who use twelve

inches for a foot and thirty-six of your inches for a yard. I am thinking that our system was clearer. But, yes, I can adapt to the British system quite easily so that is not a problem for me. You can give me any test if you are not sure.

Plus of course, I can strip down and reassemble a machine-gun blindfold in less time than it takes to down a glass of beer! So, if you're wanting someone killed in a hurry, then I'm your man!"

The foreman laughed out loud and told him to start straight away on a week's trial. Heinrich was still working there twenty years later when the factory closed down.

All seemed to be going well for Heinrich and his family when, as is so often the case with growing families, events began to spiral out of control. It was just after his son Willy had started school and the council had reinstated the annual school picnic. The war had seen an end to the end of term summer outing and, now that things had returned to normal, it was felt that it was time to resurrect the once popular event.

Previous years had involved rail trips to the seaside at Stonehaven or the pool at Tarlair near MacDuff and there had been grand picnics in the Aberdeen public parks. But budgets were tight and for the initial year at least, the plan was to hold a sports day just for primary pupils on the lower slopes of Ben Aucherie. A local farmer made a freshly harvested field available and all the local schools combined to hire coaches and charabancs and make preparations for the trip. The day before the event, the local Boy Scouts erected tents and on the day itself, a contingent of parents arrived to do the catering and hand out the sandwiches and pour the lemonade.

Sack races were duly run, an egg and spoon soon followed and there was a brave attempt at pole-vaulting across the local burn in the late afternoon. Finally, at the end of the day, the Lord Provost presented fancy medals and silver cups to the winners and the runners up.

The local paper took some finely posed photographs for the Friday lunchtime edition and to everyone's surprise, the sun kept shining and the rain stayed well out of everybody's way. It was only when the buses arrived to take the children home that the teachers did a head count and discovered that wee Willy Winkler had disappeared from the field. A search was made then a second count was carried out but there was no sign of the missing five-year-old.

Over the next three weeks, search parties and the police combed the area. Dogs were called in and at one point, there was even a search plane paid for by a national newspaper zig-zagging overhead looking for any sign of the wee lad. But to no avail. The burns were searched and the fire-ponds were dragged and every house and hen house and outhouse within five miles of the sports field was paid a visit from the searchers.

But nothing, absolutely nothing, was ever found. Not a scrap of clothing, not even a scent for the dogs and not a single trace of what became known as the wee German lad ever came to light. It was a mystery and there was no consoling his parents.

His mum Elma was the worst affected. She'd already been struggling to look after the new baby and the doctor had diagnosed depression. When several weeks went past with no sign of Willy she began to completely fall apart. She would be heard sobbing well into the night and could be found crying inconsolably throughout the day most days.

Eventually her parents stepped in to look after the baby girl and Mrs Winkler was admitted as a voluntary patient at the sanitorium in Aberdeen. After a few months she returned home apparently much improved. But it was all a charade. An inquiry was later to conclude that she had fooled the doctors and had probably stopped taking her medication as soon as she was discharged.

As far as Heinrich was concerned, he was happy to have his wife back. His son had gone forever as far as he could see and he could do nothing to change the reality of that situation. But at least with Elma back they could look after the new child and try as best as they could to move on and deal with the grief. But his wife had other ideas.

Whether it was a spur of the moment decision or a long-held plan no one would ever know. But, one evening just a few weeks following her discharge from the hospital, Heinrich came home from work to find Elma sitting alone in the semi-darkness of their kitchen. He was later to recall that there had been no tears in her eyes and that there had been a strange calmness in her demeaner.

"It was as if she had reached a decision." he would say later. "But she said nothing at first. It was only when I put the light on that she spoke to me. I think she said something like 'I'm going to sort it' or maybe it was 'I know now how to sort it'. It's all a blur now. Then she went upstairs and I heard a loud popping sound. I knew immediately what it was and rushed upstairs just in time to see her put the barrel of the gun into her mouth and pull the trigger. There was nothing, absolutely nothing I could have done!"

At the inquest it was established that whilst in a severely depressed condition following a family bereavement, Elma had become suicidal and delusional. She had taken a loaded .22 rifle normally used by Heinrich for shooting vermin and shot and killed their infant daughter before turning the gun on herself and committing suicide by shooting herself through the roof of the mouth.

Heinrich never got over the events of that night and he never forgave his wife for the sin. He continued to mourn his dead children till the end of his life and each year before the dementia took hold, on the anniversary of the disappearance of his young son, he could be found wandering the slopes of the hill near the piggery at Clart calling out the wee laddie's name as if, even after all that time had gone by, he still expected the five-year-old to emerge from the woods and come running into his arms. He blamed himself for not hiding the key to the gun cabinet though and never owned a weapon again. And he made damn sure he'd not be buried next to Elma.

Now, the mystery of what became of the child was never officially solved. There was never a body, and the wee lad's bones or clothes were never found leading to speculation that he'd been taken by a stranger. But if you asked a local even twenty years after that sad event, they'd likely say that maybe piggie got him and that he'd wandered off then stumbled and fallen in amongst the pigs at Clart. There were even some folks in the Garioch who never ate a bacon butty ever again. Just in case.

20

MR STRONACH'S PILLBOX - 28th March

Seemingly there's a street in Zimbabwe named after a one-time resident of Invermorrisay. Not that Dod ever visited Africa to verify the claim. But he did occasionally drink with the man in question and was an eager recipient of some of his swashy tales of derring do in the former British Colony. However, not long after the lad deet, a dusty document turned up in the Invermorrisay

Library Reference Collection which appeared to confirm the factoid. Replete with the odd bit of adventurous spelling, The International Gazetteer for Harare Province contained the following entry.

"Stronach Street is next to Ardbennie and is located in Harare Province, Zimbabwe. Stronach Street has a length of 0.55 kilometres. But it is splittet in separate ways."

Graeme Stronach was in his usual seat at the far end of the bar swapping bar tales with a few regulars when Dod arrived at The White Horse for his five-o-clock pint. Still wearing his winter coat and with a deer-stalker hat perched so as to cover his baldness, Graeme looked for all the world like some big land-owner or at very least a well to do farmer. But in truth, he was nothing of the sort. He was a railway engineer and had spent several decades working overseas before retiring to his native Invermorrisay.

The pub was quiet at this time of day. Just Graeme and Dave the butcher and Geordie the milkie and a middle-aged baldly lad fae Clart who'd missed his train, or at least said he had, and had obviously had a decent bucket full before he'd even gotten as far as the Horse.

The landlord, auld Jock, wis bent ahint the bar busy washing glasses wi a clorty claith which he maybe thocht wis oot o sicht. But all the regulars knew about the claith and didnae really seem tae care since the alcohol wid soon kill off all the germs and naebody ever said they got sick supping beer at The White Horse. Or, if they did, they'd maybe keep it tae themselves for fear of a telling off or even a ban.

There were plenty of stories aboot the place and most centred on auld Jock and his grippy ways. For starters, he'd had a habit of sending his wife over the road to use the public phone box if she needed to make a call since it wis cheaper than using the one in the flat above the bar. And in winter, locals knew to wrap up warm when they ventured into the place. The coal fire in the hearth would be at a peep and the central heating was only on at weekends when there was a crowd in.

If a customer dared put even a tiny shovelful of coal onto the tiny embers and was caught by Jock, he'd rant on about the price of coal and make them take it all back out again! There was even a tale about how a travelling salesman fae Penrith had complained about the bad smell in the loo and had unwisely suggested Jock maybe put some lumps of coal in the gent's urinal to soak up the stench of the urine.

"Are ye feel loon?" grumbled the old man, "dee ye no ken the price of coal?"

If your bodily needs extended beyond the urinal, you had to ask him for the key to the cubicle. It was kept out of reach behind the bar and as soon as you were back out again, auld Jock would be off to check if you'd left the loo in decent order. And, there was no toilet roll.

"Now I hinna got spare siller for toilet roll," he would tell the unfortunate customer as he handed him the sports page from the local paper along with the key.

But the conversation that particular day centred around Graeme's early career in the railways. Dod had asked him if, before he went to Africa, he'd ever worked at the Invermorrisay Locomotive Engineering Works. And of course, the answer was that he had.

Occupying a 24-acre site that backed onto the main commuter line, the factory had been constructed around the turn of the Victorian century to build and repair steam locomotives and rolling stock. The engine works quickly became the major employer in the toon and that was where, after university and a stint at the Railway Bridge Office in Aberdeen, Graeme Stronach had begun his career.

"So, what was it like back then?" asked the lad fae Clart.
"In what way?" replied Graeme. He downed the rest of his pint and turned to order a refill.
"Well what did you do?" replied the man fae Clart. "Did you work on the trains? I mean did you get to actually get tae drive one or wis you jist a ticket collector maybe?" It was a slightly silly question but required a serious answer.
"Well neither. The place was mainly a repair depot and a wagon-works. There were a few new-builds but that was before my time there. I was just out of my apprenticeship at the Bridge Office and the gaffers didn't really know what to do with me."

Graeme paused and handed Jock the money for the pint. "I mean, there was I all trained up, if you'll excuse the pun, in how to engineer a bridge. But I could hardly use a hammer never mind work on a steam engine. So, they finally put me to work as a demolition engineer."

The small group at the bar laughed.

"Yes," said Graeme. "I suppose they thought that was funny too. In my first week at the railway works, I was allocated a squad of labourers and given three days to demolish the old pillbox that guarded the factory gates. Only it didn't go quite as well as they expected."

Invermorrisay had never been attacked during the Hitler War although it must have been a tempting target for enemy bombers and the like. Alongside housing the railway works, the place was a garrison toon and the main rail and road routes North and South ran straight through the place. But, like most towns and villages up and down the East coast, the army engineers fortified the place just in case an invasion came. There were road blocks and railway barriers to slow an enemy advance and coils of barbed wire all around the place to keep locals out and keep the soldiers in. But the invasion never came and Hitler's Luftwaffe bombers were more interested in bombing the locomotive building works at Springburn and the big Clyde shipyards at Clydebank rather than the wee wagon repair works at Invermorrisay.

A big fear at the time was spies. Several had landed further North on the Buchan coast and been variously imprisoned or hung as enemy agents. But if there ever were spies in Invermorrisay, the authorities must have kept it to themselves. There were prisoners of war though. Italians and Germans and even a few Ukrainians lived in camps around the town and were encouraged, if they behaved, to make themselves useful doing farm work or digging out roads in winter. And there were pillboxes.

The pillboxes in Invermorrisay were mainly built along the line of the river bank. There were maybe seven of the things and they were built to last as Graeme Stronach was soon to discover.

"We started on the Monday and although the gaffers had allowed us three days, we were still hard at it on the Thursday although you would have been hard put to see what we'd achieved," said Graeme.

"All we had were sledge hammers and pinch bars plus a couple of hacksaws and, bear in mind these things were built to withstand bombs and bullets."

"So what did you do?" asked the inebriated man fae Clart.

"Well," said Graeme. "It was obvious that hand tools and brute strength were getting us absolutely nowhere so we asked the head gaffer if we could blow the thing up. He asked his head gaffer who asked the big boss who rang Aberdeen who rang Glasgow who agreed. It took a few days, but we had the go ahead."

"And what happened next?" said Clart.

Graeme downed the rest of his pint and ordered another.

"Well, there were no manuals in these days on how to blow up a pillbox, so had to just guess how much explosive to use. But, we really hadn't a clue and, there were no sappers amongst us. I mean none of us had ever blown up a concrete building before. But things were lax in those days so we ordered up a case of dynamite from the local quarry. It was duly delivered along with a couple of blasting workers from the council and we all went off for a liquid lunch."

"To the canteen?" asked the increasingly drunken man from Clart. Graeme paid the barman before continuing. "Well, no. Not the canteen. Although that might have been a better Idea. No, it was a Saturday afternoon and the works was closed for the weekend so we headed over to the Bakers Arms. All six of us plus one of the gaffers. And in those days, we all bought rounds. So, you can imagine the state we were in by two pm."

Seven pints, several nips and a pie later, the little demolition team headed back to the factory gate to set off the box of explosives. The blasting folk from the quarry wired the whole thing up ready to go. The local bobbies stopped the traffic on the main road and the security guard at the gate legged it to the safety of the boiler house just in case.

"We'd arranged to have the town hall warden set off the air raid siren just to be safe. But we really didn't think there would be much danger to anyone. I guess we imagined a wee puff of smoke and a wee pile of rubble waiting to be shovelled up onto the back of a lorry."

"And?" said Dave the butcher.

"Well, we all hid behind a wall until the siren went off. And then one of the quarry engineers mumbled something about God. It might have been a Hail Mary for all I know, then he pushed down the plunger and we all nearly ended up in the local cottage hospital."

There was a burst of laughter from the group of drinkers. It was Geordie the milkie who spoke first. "Was anyone killed?" he asked.

Graeme looked at him wondering what to say. It wasn't that the question was unreasonable. Just that it could maybe have been asked in a more compassionate manner. But, this after all was the man who put his nightly date with The Bill ahead of a final visit to his dying father just a few months ago. So, in the big scheme of things, what would be the point of making a scene.

"Do you maybe mean, was everybody all right Geordie?" he replied.

Geordie looked confused. "No, I wis simply askin if anyone got themselves killed in the explosion. Ah mean, was there lots of blood?"

"Well if they had been as stupid as you," came the reply "then they would probably have deserved it. But no. Nobody was killed."

The crestfallen milkie finished up his pint and ordered another. It wasn't quite time for The Bill and his mother was maybe still preparing his dinner. Graeme continued the story, embellishing it here and there with little anecdotes about how nobody was hurt and how the gaffers covered all up and how it was such a finely planned demolition and that anybody who said otherwise was talking from a place where the sun doesn't shine.

But it had been a narrow escape. The low wall that Graeme and his team were sheltering behind was all but demolished and tiny bits of concrete ended up on the roof of the boiler house and in folk's gardens more than a quarter mile away. Windows all over that part of toon were rattled by the blast and the two bobbies on the road blocks along the street were covered in dust from the explosion. A passing cat had been blown some twenty feet by the shock wave but had somehow survived. But aside from all that, and a bit of temporary deafness caused by the bang, nobody was seriously hurt and the pillbox was gone.

All that was left was a few strands of steel reinforcing rod still rooted to the concrete base and a blackened hole where the little fortress had been. The rest was just dust and rubble.

The local paper carried a report on the matter on page seven the following week. There had been a minor boiler explosion at the railway works apparently. But aside from a few rattled windows, all was well.

The missing pillbox didn't feature in the article at all. It was as though a cloud had passed and left nothing in its wake and nobody wanted to rock the boat or take the blame for the ill-planned demolition. So, the whole episode was consigned to a conspiracy of silence until that day when Mr Stronach spilled the beans at the bar at The White Horse at Invermorrisay all those years after the event.

21

THE LIBRARY SERVICE ALL FOOLS DAY STORY
COMPETITION - 1st April

Each spring, the library service would hold a competition amongst the staff for the most convincing All Fools Day story. Entries had to be submitted two weeks in advance and along with a token prize, usually chocolates or a box or two of biscuits, the winning entry would feature as a mock news item on the news pages of the Invermorrisay Weekly Herald & Post.

The Swiss Spaghetti Harvest, Big Ben Goes Digital, Viagra for Penguins and the decision by the council to approve a planning application for a lap dancing club on the summit of Ben Aucherie had already made the national headlines and the hope was that one day the library services finest might come up with something truly original. Dod entered the competition most years and on at least two occasions his articles made publication under the pseudonym April McGinty.

Despite the clue being in the name, it wasn't uncommon for irate readers to write in to the editor with comments and corrections following publication of these spurious articles. Two articles in particular raised reader's hackles. The Big Accordion Band's one-legged accordionist upset several weel kent local musicians and Dod's tale about the Hendrix Fender Strattofaster led to a torrent of letters pointing out in no uncertain terms that the editor of the newspaper should maybe be sent back to primary school to brush up on his spelling.

Wisely, Dod never publicly acknowledged ownership of this tale although his library colleagues and the staff at the local paper knew full well the true identity of April McGinty. But a few local folks suspected him and when, the following year, April McGinty again appeared in print with a piece titled "Jimi's Fender Strattofaster" both the newspaper and the library service were inundated with indignantly worded letters pointing out the various inaccuracies in the story.

Some were just in jest but it was obvious that many readers were genuinely upset that the newspaper had failed to both spell-check and fact-check the story prior to publication. In addition, a well kent Aberdeen city centre firm of auctioneers complained that they had been inundated with phone calls from collectors interested in buying the fictitious Jimi Hendrix guitar featured in the article. In response, the editor of the Herald bowed to pressure from advertisers who had threatened to boycott the paper if Ms McGinty's articles continued to be featured. And that spelled the end for the County Library Service Annual All Fools Day Story Competition.

The offending Hendrix article appeared in the local paper on the Thursday before All Fools and by the following Monday the Aberdeen City Council Housing and Infrastructure Department had received over two hundred complaints about both the misspelling of Jimi's Strattofaster guitar and the suggestion that Clapton might have played a decisive part in getting Hendrix wasted on that fateful night in 1970. Dod's one-legged accordionist tale fared little better.

22

KINLOCH'S ONE-LEGGED ACCORDIONIST
- by our special correspondent April McGinty

A special service was held at St Augustine Chapel this week to celebrate the memory of First War veteran, Laurence Taylor (1899-1949). Laurence arrived back in his native North East in the September of 1918 just a few weeks before the armistice between Germany and the Allies which effectively ended the horrific fighting that had led to the loss of millions of lives across the battlefields of Europe. After four years of trench warfare, the guns on the Western Front had finally fallen silent.

Wounded by shellfire during an abortive attack on a German redoubt near Ypres, Laurence was hospitalised for several weeks in France before being sent home to his native Kinloch where he gradually regained his strength and took stock of his new situation. Battlefield surgeons had amputated a leg below the knee and shrapnel had severed several fingers on his right hand but, despite these injuries, Laurence was determined to resume his musical career as an accordionist in a local band.

Now, folk will usually assert that there is no such thing as a left-handed accordion player. But that is not strictly the case. Given the right circumstances and a bit of determination, it is perfectly possible to play the accordion upside down. And that is exactly what Laurence trained himself to do. Over the course of several months, he not only regained his mobility but re-learned his accordion skills using an inverted keyboard specially designed for him by a local blacksmith. Over the course of several decades Laurence and The Big Accordion Band toured the UK and even made it as far as New York on one occasion becoming what was probably the very first transatlantic bothy ballad band and towards the end of his life, the lad from Kinloch was interviewed for the local paper and asked about the reason for his success.

> "It was all down to grit and determination," he told the young reporter. "And, I would do it all again if I had to! Mind you the left-handed upside-down keyboard has fairly taken its toll on my remaining fingers and you can't really toe tap effectively with just the one leg in case you fall over!"

Asked about the future he stated that he was still good enough to play the bass side but not the treble side but, with the help of a professor of musicology from the university in Aberdeen, he was working on a solution.

The years took their toll however and the man who took the bothy ballads of the North East to America eventually ended up on the streets. Fame and hangers on had taken their toll and drink had gotten a hold of him. The Big Accordion Band had long since broken up and by September 1947, the Kinloch accordionist was reduced to playing for shillings and drams in the bars and in the strip clubs of rural Aberdeenshire.

Laurence Taylor became ill on stage half way through an open-mike performance at McGinty's Bar near Cullen in 1949 and died age fifty in a Fraserburgh nursing home after a short illness. His ashes were scattered at sea. But his legacy lives on. Not least as the first left-handed accordionist to introduce doon-toon New York society to the traditional bothy ballads of the North East of Scotland.

23

JIMI'S FENDER STRATTOFASTER

- by our special correspondent April McGinty

An electric guitar once owned by Jimi Hendrix has been put up for auction in Aberdeen following a council hunt for heirs to the valuable instrument. The guitar is one of two Signature Fender Strattofaster instruments custom built for Hendrix and was used extensively by him on stage between 1967 and 1970.

The pair to this guitar was sold at auction to benefit Hendrix's canine rehabilitation charity 'Hot Chilli Dogs' in 1987. The red paper dot on the back of the headstock and the label on the accompanying case reading 'Daphne Blue 1' indicate that this particular instrument was almost certainly Hendrix's main stage guitar at The Monterey International Pop Music Festival in 1967.

The instrument was long thought to be lost and its existence only came to light when Aberdeen Council housing officer Dennis Potter was called to the home of a former council tenant to carry out a routine house clearance.

According to Mr Potter, the elderly male who had lived there for over 30 years had passed away and, with no relatives on hand to see to his affairs, it fell to the council to clear the flat and prepare it for the new tenant.

> "I was pleasantly surprised" said Dennis "to find that the place was clean and in good order."
> "It's not unusual for us to enter a property where someone has died and find that they had perhaps not been coping well during what may have been a difficult end of life period. But, in this instance, that was definitely not the case and our tenant had taken really good care of the property."

Initially, the council had assumed that relatives would come forward to claim possessions and see to the estate, but after a three-year hunt for heirs no-one came forward.

> "We were fairly certain that Mr Brown had no surviving friends in the locality," said Dennis "but we thought that maybe he had relatives somewhere who might have kept in touch at least on an occasional basis."
> "But as his birthdays came and went, there were no cards, and even at Christmas the deceased only received a few begging letters from the likes of the Chimpanzee Action Group and a charity specialising in promoting paintings made by limbless wildlife artists from North Korea."

Eventually council bosses asked Dennis to dispose of the few possessions left by the tenant and an Aberdeen auction firm was asked to provide a valuation.

> "We needed to cover the costs involved," said Dennis.
> "There was a very small amount of outstanding rent, but on top of that there was the matter of the burial and we felt we had a duty to recover what we could to protect the public purse."

The valuation however, far exceeded expectations. For in amongst the few possessions left by Mr Brown there was an electric guitar.

"I had assumed that it might be worth just a few pounds," said Dennis. "I mean, it was badly scratched, the frets looked worn and the strings had certainly seen better days. But you never know at auction since maybe someone is looking to get a real bargain."

The auctioneers were initially unimpressed with the item and consigned it to the weekly general sale in expectation that it might be worth something to someone willing to restore the neglected instrument. However, and quite by chance, musicologist Jim Hawsworthy came to preview the lots for sale.

"I couldn't believe my eyes," he explained.

"At first, I thought I was dreaming, but there right in front of me was a genuine Strattofaster! I mean these instruments are the Stradivariuses of the guitar world. There are probably only around fourteen known examples worldwide, and this one is completely genuine and original."

Seemingly Jimi Hendrix owned two of these instruments. But after his death aged 27 in September 1970, it emerged that one was unaccounted for.

In a strange twist, it transpired that the deceased Mr Brown had been drinking red wine with Marmalade stars Gary Farr and Jimmy Cregan, together with Eric Clapton at the Scotch of St James bar in Mayfair on the evening of Hendrix's death.

"When Jimi came in," recalled Clapton, "he had no dosh on him whatsoever and neither had the rest of us cause we'd spent it all at the bar and had a tab running. So, we asked Bennie Brown the roadie to bung us a few quid. Just to keep the party going you understand. He wasn't best pleased though and he got a bit agitated cause we never usually repaid him."

"By that time the bar bill was astronomical and to be honest we was all a bit keen to get more wasted. So, to calm Bennie down, I suggested that we bung him a guitar as collateral. That's how it all happened really. He was pleased as punch and went off strumming Jimi's guitar.

I know that because I was there. Or at least I think I was. And we all had some outrageous fun that night as far as I can remember. That is until I awoke to find that Jimi had, well you know, gone off somewhere and died basically. Never forget that night really. What year is it today anyway?"

Be that as it may, the auction of the Hendrix Strattofaster takes place at Aberdeen Central Auction House on May 2nd next with all proceeds going directly to the council.

The sales catalogue reads as follows:

LOT NUMBER 405
FENDER STRATTOFASTER, JIMI HENDRIX SIGNATURE MODEL, circa 1967
Serial number CZ510969, maple tarnished finish, maple neck with skunk-stripe routing, red paper dot on back of headstock beside "Sandy Klaus Fender Custom Shop" transfer, twenty-two fret fingerboard with dot inlays, three pre-Vintage Noiseless pickups, three rotary controls, selector switch, tremolo/bridge tail block and white pick guard; and a black Harry Fender hard-shell bright-contour case with black plush lining and cream cloth sticker inscribed in hazy purple felt pen *"Good luck Jimi from your good old pals Otis, Eric and Shanker"* and tie on paper label inscribed on both sides in black felt pen "FENDER STRAT CZ510969 MAPLE 1", one red and one green paper dot on two case latches."

A reserve price of £24,500 has been placed on the item and international interest is expected.

———————————

Dod wis fair chuffed aboot the fact that his wee April McGinty articles had made it into print even if there wis nae truth in them at all. And, he had only another 1,219 days to go till he could finally retire from his shackles at the Invermorrisay Public Library.
Aye!

VOCABULARY

aa *adj.* all

aat *pr.* that

affrontit *ppl., adj.* ashamed

ahint *adv.* behind

Aiberdeen *place name.* Aberdeen

airse *n.* arse

an *conj.* and

aroon *adv.* around

auld *adj.* old

ava *adj.* at all

awa *adv.* away

bather *v.* bother

bidie-in *n.* live in lover

blin *adj.* blind

bobbie *n.* policeman

brae *n.* steep road

breeks *n.* trousers

brig *n.* bridge

Buchan *place name.* Administrative area of North East Scotland

caal *adj.* cold

chaep *adj.* cheap

chik *n.* cheek

colourfu *adj.* colourful

claith *n.* cloth

clorty *adj.* dirty

dee *v.* do

deet *v. pt.* died

deil *n.* devil

deuk *n.* duck

dinna *v.neg.* don't

dockit *ppl.* docked or cut short

doot *n.* doubt

Dod *nickname.* George

doon *adv.* down

drabbly *adj.* wet

dreepin *n.* dripping

drookit *adj.* drenched

droon *v.* drown

dunderheid *n.* fool

ee *pron.* you

fae *prep.* from

fairm *n.* farm

feel *n.* fool

fit like? *phrase.* how are you?

float *n.* livestock transport vehicle

fou *adj.* full

gaffer *n.* foreman

Garioch geographical area in Aberdeenshire. From the Gaelic *Gairbheach* (place of roughness)

gaun on *phrase.* going on

geen *v.* gone

grippy *adj.* stingy

grunter *n.* pig

guid *adj.* good

hae *v.* have

hairmless *adj.* harmless

het *adj.* hot

hinna *v. neg.* have not

ill-trickit *adj.* mischievous

ither *adj.* other

lang *adj.* long

loon *n.* lad

lum *n.* chimney

mair *adj.* more

maist *adj.* most

mannie *n.* man

mart *n.* building used for auctions

Mearns *place name.* geographical area of Kincardineshire

micht *n.* might

milkie *n.* milkman

mither *n.* mother

nae *adj.* no

naebody *pro.* Nobody

nary a drop *phrase.* not a single drop

nicht *n.* night

nip *n.* a measure of whisky

ower *adj.* over

pintie *n.* imperial pint measure (often milk or beer)

pure gallus *phrase.* excellent

quine *n.* girl

roon aboot *phrase.* round about

sair *adj.* sore

shebeen *n.* informal unlicenced drinking establishment

Sheen *n.* shoes

sicht *n.* sight

siller *n.* money

skinnymalinky *adj.* thin

skweels *n.* schools

skunnered *adj.* annoyed

sleepin *n.* sleeping

soo *n.* sow (aka grumphie or grunter)

stane *n.* stone

stovies *n.* a stew of cooked potatoes with onion and meat scraps

St Tibb's Eve a festival that is never going to happen

swashy *adj.* grand

tae *prep.* to

tak *v.* take

The Broch *place name.* local name for the town of Fraserburgh

thocht *n.* thought

thon *pr.* that

toon *n.* town

tummle-doon *adj.* tumble down

unca fu *phrase.* very drunk/steaming

wairmer *n.* warmer

wantin *adj.* wanting

weel *exclamation.* well (also **nae weel** *phrase.* unwell)

weel kent *phrase.* well known

weet *adj.* wet

wi *prep.* with

wid *v.* would

wik *n.* week

Willum *nickname.* William

wird *n.* word

ye *pron.* you

BIBLIOGRAPHY

Aberdeen Voice. *Various editions 2010 onwards* (Community owned digital newspaper – editor Fred Wilkinson)

Aitken, Margaret. *Six Buchan Villages* (Self-published circa 1975)

Aitken, Margaret. *Six Buchan Villages* (Scottish Cultural Press 2004)

Alexander, William. *Johnny Gibb of Gushetneuk in the Parish of Pyketillim* (David Douglas, Edinburgh, 1880)

Anderson, James. *The Black Book of Kincardineshire* (Johnston 1853)

Anson, Peter. *The Caravan Pilgrim* (Cranton 1938)

Bailies of Bennachie. *Bennachie Again* (William Culross and Son 1983)

Balfour, Bernard. *Secrets, Stories, Memories and Stones* (Cranstone 1993)

Barclay, Gordon. *If Hitler Comes* (Padstow 2013)

Braemar Gathering Annual – Various (Dee Publishing)

Burnett, Allan. *Duff House at War* (Aberdeenshire Council, unknown date)

Campbell, Valerie. *Camp 165 Watten: Scotland's Most Secretive POW Camp* (Whittles Publishing 2007)

Chorlton, Martyn. *Scottish Airfields Vol.3* (Countryside 2010)

Christie, Elizabeth. *The Empty Shore* (Bruce 1974)

Christie, Elizabeth. *The Haven under the Hill – The Story of Stonehaven* (Bruce 1977)

Cunningham, Tom. *Your Fathers the Ghosts* (Black & White 2007)

Davidson, John. *Inverurie and the Earldom of the Garioch* (A. Brown & Co 1878)

D-Maps: https://d-maps.com/

Duff, David. *Queen Victoria's Highland Journals* (Lomond Books 1998)

Fenton, Alexander. *The Turra Coo* (Aberdeen University Press 1989)

Ferguson, David. *Shipwrecks of North East Scotland* (Aberdeen University Press 1991)

Forsyth, F. *The Day of the Jackal* (Various)

Gordon Forum for the Arts. *In Celebration of Inverurie* (Culross - no date)

Grampian Regional Council. *A Historical Walk Around Peterhead* (School Resources Department 1998)

Hamilton, Sheila. *What's in a name* (Aberdeen Journals Ltd 1986)

Harley, Duncan. *The A-Z of Curious Aberdeenshire* (The History Press 2017)

Harley, Duncan. *The Little History of Aberdeenshire* (The History Press 2019)

Harley, Duncan. *The Poetry Mannie* (KDP Press 2022)

Harley, Duncan. *Long Shadows* (KDP Press 2020)

Isherwood and Welsh. *Deeside Donside and Angus* (Clan Books 2004)

Kilbride-Jones, FE. *An Account of the Excavation of the Stone Circles at Loanhead of Daviot* (H.M. Office of Works)

Kynoch, Douglas. *A Doric Dictionary* (Luath Press 2022)

Leopard Magazine. *Various editions* (Aberdeen University/Judy Mackie editor)

Mackie, Alexander. *Aberdeenshire* (Cambridge University Press 1911)

Marren, Peter. *Grampian Battlefields* (Mercat Press 1990)

McConnachie, Alex Inkson. *Donside* (James G. Bisset 1900 edition)

McGinty, Stephen. *Fire in the Night.* (Macmillan 2008)

McKean, Charles. *Banff and Buchan- an Illustrated Guide* (Mainstream 1990)

Meldrum, Edward. *Aberdeen of Old* (Rainbow 1993)

Morgan, Diane. *Various including Footdee* (Highland Printers Inverness 1993)

Osborne, Mike. *Defending Britain* (The History Press 2011)

Osborne, Dod – *Master of the Girl Pat* (Country Life Press 1923)

Pittock, Murray. *A New History of Scotland* (Sutton Publishing 2002)

Porter and Williams. *Epidemic Diseases in Aberdeen and the History of the City Hospital* (Polestar 1971)

Robb, William. *Victorian Scenes* (Keith and District Heritage Group circa 1980)

Rowe, Anthony. *The Brown Caravan* (Cranton 1935)

Shepherd, Ian. *Exploring Scotland's Heritage* (Her Majesty's Stationary Office 1986)

Shepherd, Mike. *Oil Strike North Sea* (Luath Press 2016)

Shepherd, Mike. *When Brave Men Shudder: The Scottish Origins of Dracula* (Wild Wolf Publishing 2018)

Smith, Robert. *Discovering Aberdeenshire* (John Donald Publishers 1998)

Smith, Robert. *Land of the Lost* (Birlinn1997)

Smith, Robert. *The Road to Maggieknockater* (Birlin 2004)

Stewart, Alan. *North East Scotland at War* (Self Published 2018)

Swan, Eddi. *His Majesty's Theatre – One Hundred Years of Glorious Damnation* (Black & White Publishing 2006)

Tacitus. *Agricola* (Various AD 83)

Taylor, Les. *Luftwaffe over Scotland* (Whittles 2013)

The Bailies of Bennachie. *The Book of Bennachie* (William Culross & Son 1976)

The Buchan Heritage Society. *Heirship '94* (The Buchan Heritage Society 1994)

Thomson, Arthur. *The North-East* (Aberdeen University Press 1930)

Toulmin, David. *Straw into Gold* (Impulse Books Aberdeen 1973)

Toulmin, David. *The Tillycorthie Story* (University of Aberdeen 1986)

Vallance, Hugh. *The Great North of Scotland Railway* (David St John 1991)

Vonnegut, K. *Slaughterhouse-Five* (Various)

Watt, Brian. *Old Stonehaven* (Stanlake Publishing 2000)

Watt, William. *A History of Aberdeen and Banff* (William Blackwood 1900)

Webster, Jack. *Jack Webster's Aberdeen* (Birlinn Books Ltd 2007)

Wood, Sydney. *The Shaping of Aberdeenshire* (SPA Books 1985)

Wyness, Fenton. *Royal Valley* (Reid 1968)

ABOUT THE AUTHOR

Image courtesy of Gail McMillan

Duncan Harley has written extensively about the history and the mythology of the North East of Scotland. He worked for a time at a well-known street newspaper before taking up free-lance writing and photography. Feature writing now takes up much of his time alongside the penning of both theatrical and literary reviews. Duncan lives in rural Aberdeenshire and is surrounded by a huge pile of other people's books. At weekends and holidays, he likes nothing better than to explore the history and the landscape of his native Scotland.

Also available from Amazon and all good booksellers:

Printed in Great Britain
by Amazon